THE OMNIST AND THE COSMIC EGG

BOOK THREE IN THE OMNIST SERIES

ROB WELDON

This is the one. This one is real. This is so much realer than the other times. Those were all part of my condition. Now I really know what it's like to die.

    – William Oxford

Colors don't need us. Words don't need us. Or music. Nobody gives us these. It's their world and they let us live in it.

    – Lucid Oxford

A common mistake is thinking a turtle and its shell are separate.

    – Cara Pace

If words exist outside us, then words like "life" and "death" are hollow until they land on someone.

    – Raine Oxford

I've heard people argue about which existed first: matter or energy. I believe math existed before both. It's the skeleton that holds up the flesh of everything else, including music.

    – Jacob Feynman

CHAPTER
ONE

1. WILLIAM

I t was the weirdest thing.

He'd skipped breakfast this morning, telling Olivia he had to be at the office early. She'd made breakfast sandwiches with egg, spinach, cheese, and his favorite secret ingredient: a combination of Thousand Island dressing and hot sauce. Normally, William would've been all over it. He did actually feel bad for not joining her.

"What's wrong?" Olivia had said when he was at the door, about to leave.

"Just work stuff," he said.

She looked worried. "You're not mad, are you?"

"There's nothing to be mad about." He meant this. "Only thankful. We'll talk later."

She rose up on her tiptoes, expecting their usual goodbye

kiss, but he was hesitant. She'd know. What if he felt cold to her? He leaned down and pecked her softly on the cheek, slipping out the door as quickly as he could without garnering more questions. She didn't seem to notice.

Some people felt dead in the morning. Or wished they were. He'd had his share of hangovers. *Act like you've been here before.* This wasn't a hangover. He'd gone to bed early last night, feeling weighed down, the heaviest his body had ever felt. His brain had felt too swollen for his cranium, and sleep was the only thing that would help.

But what Olivia hadn't realized was that William had died in his sleep. Or he woke up dead. Whatever. Dead people didn't eat breakfast. Unlike the common cliché, they didn't eat brains, either. They didn't eat anything. They were dead.

He'd showered, though. And wore deodorant and dressed properly. He wasn't an animal. Besides, when he began to rot, the scent of Tuscan Leather would buy him a little more time. He'd thrown a travel-sized ten-ML bottle of Cuneiform Cure cologne and a stick of Dry-Aged Spices deodorant in the pocket of his computer bag, just in case, both items purchased from Consumia's Spiritual Emporium. Their story cards had promised they would ward off evil spirits while providing a pleasing aroma, or something to that effect. Bad smells were evil, obviously.

He didn't know what else to do, so he drove to the office and continued with his routine for now, albeit food-free. This was bonus time, an extended life, like that granted to a player in an old arcade video game. If he went to a hospital, they would confirm his status and not let him leave. He wasn't ready to be carted down to the morgue, lie still, and be awake until his eyes and brain rotted away. He'd heard liquefaction occurred relatively quickly, within a few days, and that just didn't sound fun.

He could make a few calls at his desk. Do some paperwork while he could still function. Act normal while he thought of what to do next.

But why? If it was only a matter of time before his body grew bloated and full of maggots, he'd rather get a round of golf in. He didn't know how long his memory would function, but a fade-out on something recent and pleasant seemed like the way to go.

He decided he'd set up at the office and ask Phil to play. Nobody else in the world seemed to understand him as well, so it would be fine as a closing memory.

~

GETTING Phil to agree to a round wasn't difficult. Phil asked him to shoot at least twice a week, and half the time William said no, he was too busy with work. But just in case, William always kept a set of sticks in the trunk of his car. They could crunch numbers well into the night, but golf relied on sunlight. Some things took priority.

An hour later, they were at the course. The employees there were familiar with Phil, and he'd been known to slip someone a Franklin to be squeezed in when tee times were otherwise full.

Great weather. Sunny. Bright. Lots of shade trees. Not too hot yet.

Yes, this felt like the place to be.

~

SEVERAL YEARS AGO, William had been considering leaving Feltson & Associates to strike out on his own. He'd been there ten years, and it was time. He'd been afraid of Phil Feltson finding out before anything was finalized, but other than side-eye glances from others at the office and a few exaggerated pleasantries that triggered his paranoia, nobody said anything to him.

They'd been at this very course, and before the fourth hole, a beautiful tree-shaded par five, the foursome behind them far behind and not encroaching anytime soon, when Phil produced an expensive bottle of scotch from his bag and looked at it admiringly.

"What's that for?" William said. Phil was more likely to drink after a round, not during.

"I carry this, the eighteen-year, to celebrate when someone leaves the company."

So, Phil did know. At least he brought out the good stuff. But William had only told Geta and his dad. Geta was the leak; she had to be.

"Who's leaving?" William said. *Make him say it.*

"But I've been looking at it wrong," Phil said, ignoring his question. "Really though, a five-hundred-dollar bottle should be broken out when there's cause for celebration." Phil took out two tumblers and handed one to William. He poured two fingers into each. "Celebrating big life changes."

"Of course," William said. *Right. Leaving your job is definitely a big life change.*

Phil held up his glass to the sun. It was nicer crystal than William had at home. And this was what Phil kept in his golf bag. "You're supposed to make me a toast," he said.

"I am, huh? Oh, okay then," William said, thinking quickly. "Here's to all your future pars becoming birdies, so that they fly low to the score." It was off the cuff, best he could do. In a situation like this, it was preferrable to play dumb, but sound confident.

"Not what I expected you to say," Phil said. "I thought you'd know what I was getting at. You know how word travels around the office. It's like the walls have ears, the doors have eyes."

Typical Phil. Cryptic as fuck. *Make him say it.*

William's arm was tiring from holding up the glass away from his body, mid-toast. This was like waiting for a kiss from your executioner. The sun refracted in the crystal glass in such a way that William had to turn his body a little, rather than lower the glass.

"Maybe it's better this way," Phil said. "I started this company with a small inheritance in my twenties. And now I'm making the first toast as it evolves into the new firm: Feltson and Oxford, LLP."

William was confused at first, but caught on quickly. His boss was confident and presumptuous enough to think that William would agree to being made partner. William liked that. It turned out he'd be a minority partner, but his name would be on the door. And Phil was right; he agreed immediately.

Nonetheless, William's golf game deteriorated throughout the round as the bottle drained, and overall, he didn't play very well. He didn't need to. At the end they sat in the clubhouse, more to hydrate and sober up in the air conditioning than to get another drink.

So instead of divorcing his company of ten years, William divorced his first wife, Geta, of twenty.

THE QUESTION NOW WAS, do you tell Phil you're dead? And if so, how? If an act of nature came into play, like flies buzzing in his mouth or blackbirds attacking his eyes, the answer would be unquestionably yes. Easy math.

There would be no roving wet bar in Phil's golf bag today. It'd be a normal round, with work to follow, so William wouldn't have to fake-drink in front of him. Dead people didn't drink, either.

An ambassador in a golf cart escorted them to the first tee, where she told the foursome that was scheduled for the current timeslot to allow Phil and William to play through ahead of them. Since the course didn't officially allow twosomes, the gesture seemed to impart some presumed importance. So, after handshakes all around and phony encouragements from the others, Phil gave William the honors.

William felt four sets of resentful eyes burning holes into him as he set to tee off. His muscles tightened. He reminded himself to relax. Dead people could relax. That was by definition.

They could also tighten up.

He shanked the ball off to the right.

"Drop a provisional," someone from the other party said. It made sense. Why play a ball that had only traveled forty yards, barely inbounds, which would likely lead to a double bogey, when he could hit the next one straight for two hundred and ninety? The round wasn't going to start until they said it started.

"Yeah, shake it off," another golfer said. "Hit another."

His redo turned out fine. An average shot for him.

Then, a few minutes later, he shanked a chip shot. "I'm dead today," he muttered, before he knew he'd said it.

"Meh, you're just in your head too much," Phil said. By comparison, *his* play was on point.

By the fourth hole, the one where he'd been made partner five years ago, William noticed he was sweating a lot for a dead person. Then again, his body had cooled. Set a glass of ice water in a humid room and watch how much it sweats. You don't need to be alive to have moisture condense on you.

WILLIAM TRIPLE-PUTTED, which meant he'd bogeyed all six of the first holes. At least he was consistent in death.

"You're right," Phil said. "You're off today."

"I'm afraid I'm not going to improve," William said. "It's all downhill from here."

"Don't be so hard on yourself."

"Phil, listen to me," he said. "I don't know who else to tell... but...I died last night." That sounded far worse out loud than it had in his head. "You have to believe me."

"You'll shake it off."

"No, seriously. I'm dead. I died in my sleep last night."

"I don't know what drugs you're taking, but I want some. Or give some to my neighbor's dog so I can sleep."

"Honest." William held up a ball that had a smudge of green on it. He put it in a ball washer and pumped the handle a few times. "This is probably my last round ever. I just want to enjoy it."

"I've died in my dreams before, too. Freaks me out, but then I go back to sleep. I'm fine the next day."

"Let me ask you a question," William said. Instead of drying the ball on the dirty towel hanging from the cleaner, he used his own hand towel hanging off his bag. "How do you know you're really alive?"

"I don't know, I have a pulse. That's one." Phil grabbed

William's wrist and closed his eyes. "So do you. Done. What do you think of that?"

"I think..." William's mind flashed through a hundred thoughts, none of them providing the answer. "It means..." Memories, forgotten memories, people he knew, lies, truths, close calls with death. "Dead people can have a pulse."

CHAPTER
TWO

2. LUCADOR

Lucador often enjoyed startling regular customers as they came through the front door of Omnist II, jumping off a riser with his sword aloft.

"HaHAA!" he would say in his trademark rebel yell. It worked. People were startled.

"Can you find something else to do?" Kick asked, startled, as he adjusted the towel for catching spills under the nozzle of a cistern. He'd inadvertently shaken the vessel when Lucador had jumped, causing the ice to rattle inside. It was a spicy iced-tea-and-fruit beverage, a sort of caffeinated punch flavored with jalapeño and floating pieces of strawberries and raspberries. Lucador enjoyed it. They sold tea there at Omnist II, as well, blends made by local artisans, but this was an Omnist II original creation, free for guests.

"We've slayed the dragon of inventory, so now is the time for play." Lucador re-perched himself on the corner of the stage riser closest to the door to await his next victim. From his new height, he lifted his chin and caught a blurry glimpse of himself in his blade. His sideburns were shaved to sharpened sword-like points along his jawline, and were momentarily angled parallel to his personally forged weapon.

"I can't believe I've partnered with a child," Kick said.

"Child?" Lucador couldn't believe this, either. "I am a man! I lead the masses! A mentor to my flock! A father!"

"I'm sorry, Luc." Kick stacked boxes of ceramic-and-wood Omnist II tiki mugs between the cistern and the paper cups. The mugs' story cards were stamped with a red Omnist II logo and announced a price of only twenty dollars. Lucador approved of Kick's product placement. "I just can't imagine you with a child. Jumping at them with a weapon?"

Lucador didn't jump at everyone, of course. Just people he was familiar with, or who looked like they were asking for it. So when a lanky twenty-one-year-old entered the store not asking for it, he didn't jump at him. The kid looked like he would dissolve into a puddle of fear, and no one should be dissolving at a shop built for champions.

The young man appeared caught in an awkward-teen stage of physical development. If he shaved at all, it was likely because he felt the stubble more than anyone saw it. No sharpened facial weapons for him yet. He walked to the counter where Kick was standing.

"Hi, Lucid," Kick said. "Here to watch the playoffs?"

Kick, mid-thirties, was a technology nerd and esports fan who'd demanded several large flatscreens be affixed to the exposed brick walls of Omnist II, plus seating areas for fans to watch live esports on Flinch TV. There was a streamed event this afternoon, which would draw a dozen or so extra bodies into the store.

Lucid looked above the heads of the two employees, then up at a screen.

"The baby brother of the Raine-y day, the sprinkle, the drizzle," Lucador said, lowering the sword. Lucador was in his early forties, and considered himself a real-life video game hero. *If you live like a victor, you'll always be a victor.* He work-shopped a lot of ideas, some of them conflicting. But Lucador was nobody's little brother, literally or figuratively. Raine was Lucid's older sister. "I saw your sister at the Emporium yester-day, and she spread to me the news." The Emporium was a reference to Consumia's Spiritual Emporium, their flagship store. "So, I brought you a present."

Apparently, the commentary warranted no response. Lucid stood silently, waiting or thinking. It wasn't stoicism, as Lucid was prone to overreactions. This was just everyday unrespon-siveness. Lucador sheathed his weapon and went to the back room—or the Forgery, as he called it—where there was a mini-refrigerator for employee personal items, and removed a plastic resealable bag with an egg in it.

"HaHAA!" he said when he returned, holding up the gift. Both Kick and Lucid had begun watching Flinch TV on one of the screens, where a first-person fighting game was in progress. "Kick wouldn't let me keep this in the fridge out here." Lucador was referring to the glass-door refrigerator wall that displayed locally produced bottled iced tea, kombucha, organic sodas, herbs, olives, and pickled vegetables. There were some food spells and potions, as well, that imbued the consumer with qualities like courage, patience, or intelligence.

"It's only for customer stuff," Kick said. "You know this."

"It's my refrigerator, too, but I digress!" Lucador removed

the egg and tossed the bag on the counter. "I heard you like the eggs," he said to Lucid.

"I guess." Lucid hadn't changed expressions since arriving. His eyes followed the oblong shape in Lucador's hands.

"Eggs are good. Good thing to like." Lucador shook the egg by his ear as if listening for a rattle or some other telltale sign of its quality. "Here, take this."

Lucid didn't move.

"Hold out your hand!" Lucador's uncontrolled volume seemed to make Lucid more hesitant. Lucid gingerly held out his hand. Lucador placed the egg there reverently, and Lucid's hand dipped a couple inches as if the egg were made of lead. "Now close your hand," Lucador said. "Try to squeeze. Hard as you can."

"But it'll break." Lucid made a soft fist around it.

"No, it won't. It's too strong," Lucador said. "You have the strength, but you can't do it."

Lucid looked scared.

"Just do it! Squeeze it like the blood from the stone!"

Lucid made a face as he squeezed and the egg didn't break. Lucador sandwiched Lucid's fist between his own hands and pressed hard, combining their strength.

"HaHAA! See?" he said. "Doesn't break! Now open it up!"

When Lucid opened his hand, exposing the egg, Lucador struck down like he was slapping him five, splattering and squishing raw egg all over both of their hands before locking them in a messy handshake. He kept a grip on Lucid's hand and shook it as a business partner would, enthusiastically sealing the deal. Lucid was trembling like his legs were about to give out. Scared. Weak.

"But see? We succeed!" He lifted their dripping hands in victory. "We're bigger than the egg. Stronger! Not playing by the egg's rules!"

"Luc, what the hell?" Kick said. "You're going to clean that up, right?"

"Some things you cannot do alone." Lucador let go and looked at their hands, the strands of egg slipping between their fingers, with large flakes of shell sliding to the floor.

Lucid was out of breath, like he'd just witnessed an act of violence, a mugging or a stabbing. "What...do...you..." he said.

"What do I *want?* HaHAA!" Lucador felt this couldn't be going any better.

"Luc, leave him alone." Kick put a reassuring hand on Lucid's shoulder, which

seemed to add too much weight. Lucid leaned forward and put his clean hand on a knee, steadying himself. "Are you okay?" Kick said.

"...*mean?*" Lucid was struggling to find the words, or the breath with which to say them. "Not to...walk on...eggshells?"

"No!" Lucador stomped his foot in the mess. One egg wasn't a large amount of volume, but little bits of shell crunched, and the albumen and yolk made a squishy vacuum sound when he lifted his leather boot.

There weren't many customers in the store, but every one of them was watching, including two uber-relaxed teenagers draped on sectional couches in the No-Basil Alcove, the audience area Lucador aptly named in juxtaposition to CSE's Basil Alcove. There was a couple who'd just entered through the front door, two women browsing in an aisle, and a man standing at the counter waiting for Kick to ring him up.

"Damn it, dude, stop!" Kick rarely raised his voice.

"Don't worry, Kick, I won't slip!" Lucador stomped again, transforming the moves into his interpretation of a flamenco dance that backed him a couple feet away.

"Ignore him," Kick said to Lucid, helping ease him down the rest of the way to the floor where he sat himself, hyperventilating. The weight on Lucid's shoulders looked heavy, like he was ready to lie in a fetal position and die amid the broken egg.

There was a display near them for Lucador's homemade beef jerky, with tongs to lift pieces into small, white paper bags, and Kick grabbed a bag, opened it, and put the opening up to Lucid's mouth. "Take deep breaths," Kick said. "I know, a bigger bag would be better."

Lucid gasped inconsistently into the bag for a couple moments, then his breathing leveled out, deep and steady.

"Don't worry, your body won't let you die." Lucador rubbed the top of Lucid's hair, wiping egg from his hand into it. "Egg is good for you. Good for the hair."

"Stop that!" Kick said, knocking Lucador's arm away. "Will you go help Max?"

Lucador lit up. "Ah, Max! The gardens of the valley will feed the masses!"

Max, looking confused, set a premade salad and a boxed role-playing game on the counter. Kick knew him better than Lucador did. Max was a fellow gamer with tattoos of victorious characters to give him strength.

"Vegan gamers, they eat, too!" Lucador said. "That's what I meant!"

"Right," Max said. He was paying more attention to Kick and Lucid than his purchase.

"You have kind words," Lucid said, looking all around and above Kick's head. "They choose to be with you." Kick helped him up and patted him on the back as he shuffled away.

"Not afraid to spill the blood," Lucador said to Max, ringing up the game. Then he picked up and shook the salad. "But that doesn't mean you eat the blood!"

"Nope." Max seemed accustomed to the uniqueness of Omnist II and its employees. He waved with his salad. "Kick," he said as an exit greeting and left the store.

Why would Lucid say kind words choose to be with Kick? He'd never said anything like that to Lucador before.

"Seriously, Luc," Kick said. "Do you even have the capability to see things from someone else's perspective?"

"The boy, the Lucid, he is stronger now. Watch!" Lucador said.

"And that empathy thing we've talked about? Kind of need that to see things from the customer's perspective."

"Phooey!"

"Seriously. Jumping at customers with a weapon?"

"Everybody loves that!" Lucador said. "You say that's why we're partners! The swords come with the deal. They're part of me. And I only jump at friends; you see this. I left the Lucid alone. He's family."

"That's because you had other plans for him."

"One plan. One egg. It's done. Now you watch!" Lucador poured a spicy fruit tea into a carved wooden tiki mug. "I'll cheer him up. With this!" He held up the mug triumphantly.

"Ooh, with a free Arnold Palmer?" Kick said. "Will he have to wear that, now, too?"

"He's a good kid. Just needs a break out of the shell."

Lucador was admittedly still getting used to the customer service aspect of owning one third of a store. Kick and Connie each owned the other thirds. Connie had founded Consumia's Spiritual Emporium in North Hollywood, with Kick owning a minority piece. Kick ran much of the technological side, mainly their app called the Omnist. Lucador was the most popular Omniscian at CSE and sold a lot of merchandise, and in many ways had outgrown the flagship store. He and Kick wanted a new location to give him more space for his merchandise and more time for his Lodges. Lucador loved Omnist II's location. Echo Park was in the shadow of downtown, a grittier location, older, and populated with the souls of the founders of Los Angeles.

One morning, just after the new store had opened for business, Lucador and Kick had stood out front on the sidewalk, checking the window dressing, the traffic on Sunset Boulevard heavy. Lucador watered a planter box, then sucked in the air, expanding his chest out and over his stomach. "Smell that?" he said. "I love the smell of Echo Park in the morning."

"All I smell is piss," Kick had said. There was that, too.

He knew Kick liked it here. Lucador's co-owner had only said that to rile him up. But he wouldn't take the bait. It was he who would do the riling.

CURRENTLY, Kick rolled out a yellow mop bucket. "Here you go. I'm not doing this."

"No, no, no, no. You watch!" Lucador took the handle and leaned it against his chest like he was going to dance with it. "But we wait for the Lucid."

"Are you going to apologize to him before Raine comes bursting in here later?"

"No, no, no, no. You watch!" Lucador swished the water around. It was all going to plan.

"You said that already. Like four times."

"The lessons, they write themselves," Lucador said. "And I write the lessons!"

"Can you even break an egg that way?" Kick said. "By squeezing it in your palm?"

"I use the side of a Mayan bowl. Makes a good omelet.

Jalapeños, tomatoes, onions...cheese." He imagined using a razor-sharp scimitar on a cutting board, rocking it back and forth along its curve, chopping vegetables. Fine mincing.

No, he would never do that. He wasn't crazy.

CHAPTER
THREE

3. RAINE

"Why are you home? I thought you were gracing Omnist II with your presence tonight," Raine said. She presented herself in a no-makeup, no-hair-product, and certainly no-camera-filter way. Her hair was long and straight, naturally dark blonde or light brown, depending on the light, and was often held in place with two antique barrettes. But not now, not at home. Behind her ears held well enough.

Lucid's hair was damp and flat, like he'd recently stepped out of the shower. And it wasn't raining. He usually kept his hair pointed in as many directions as possible, to point it at as many flelling words as possible. He didn't look happy.

"Did you opt to take another shower or did a shower take you?" she said.

No response.

He wasn't just unhappy. Lucid was pissed. If he'd been holding something he would've slammed it on the couch, as he made that motion anyway. "Why'd you tell him about eggs?" he said, voice wavering. "My eggs! Not your eggs to talk about!"

Of course, anybody could talk about eggs: ovaries, baby chickens, omelets. But ownership of the concept of eggs and their underlying role in the universe seemed, to Lucid, to belong to him alone. He even slept in one.

It was Raine's turn not to respond. She was the "normal" one in her family. Besides the egg thing, her little brother saw words everywhere and unique colors in everything.

"I knew something was afoot as soon as I left here," he said, changing gears. "The sky was greyer and less purple, which made the grass redder. The sprinklers, orange." He paused, then corrected himself. "Tangerine!"

This was supposed to mean something to Raine, but she usually gauged his moods on other clues than the colors he said he saw. Things like his energy, posture, tone of voice, vocabulary, et cetera. For him, talking about purple-tinged air wasn't a joke about wearing "rose-tinted glasses," an expression that likely made no sense to him.

Then again, he'd said he felt social today and wanted out of his shell. He'd said he'd use his egg tooth, a figurative piece of bone on his upper lip, to break himself free. He claimed to be one of the only people on the planet born with this much-needed physiological tool. He didn't have an egg tooth, of course, but Raine always let that slide. Without encouraging him, necessarily, she allowed him some freedoms with reality if they helped him express how he was feeling and to overcome his fears.

To the uninitiated, Lucid seemed inconsistent in his

descriptions of the world. But his color schemes seemed to have an internal, intuitive logic. His perception of colors served as a sort of mood ring. Like seeing the air as tie-dyed, his moods just had more flair than other people's.

Today Lucid wore an oversized bright purple T-shirt, tan work pants, and red canvas shoes. He often wore interesting color "matches," items others wouldn't think to combine. For someone who said he didn't care how he looked, he was picky about what he wore.

Raine would've liked to live in a color palette from the 1960s. People had often accused her of living in the wrong decade for years, saying that she was an old soul, a sort of new age modern hippie. So maybe the two siblings weren't all that different.

"It's your fault," he said after a moment.

"Can you share what happened?"

"Egg!" Lucid grabbed a lock of his hair and pulled on it. "Egg in my hair!"

WHEN RAINE and Lucid were in junior high school, some neighborhood kids egged their house, the thuds sounding like distant bombs exploding. She'd run to the window and heard the kids laughing as they rode off on their bicycles.

As a family, they went outside to look, staring at the house, feeling violated. Lucid was visibly shaking. The sun had gone down, but with the way the light from the magic-hour sky hit the runny new coating, it seemed to glow.

"They're just eggs," Dad had said.

"They're words," Raine said, looking over at a subdued Lucid.

"And words can never hurt you," Mom said.

Even Raine knew that wasn't true. Experiencing other children's cruelty at school toward her and Lucid for being different, she'd learned that somehow the words for sticks and stones were mightier than the sword.

She learned that for Lucid, if eggs represented words and a picture was worth a thousand words, those eggs said much more shattered into multicolored frescos on their walls than the kids could have said with their mouths or fists. In order to calm down afterward, Lucid had needed Raine to lie on his back while they listened to a stream of a classical music.

He was only a year and a half younger, but even as children, he seemed like Raine's son. Or rather, she felt like his mother. She was twenty-two now, and he'd just turned twenty-one. He was born Lewis, named after their paternal grandfather, but went by the nickname Lucid. Firstly, because of his technicolor, day-glow descriptions of things as a child, then secondly, because social media and gaming took hold. In the last five years he'd used variations of Luc1dEgg, LUC1Ddr3am, et cetera, as usernames. But he was Lucid among the people that knew him.

RAINE CURRENTLY SAW her phone light up next to her. It was a text from Jacob. She didn't mean to look; it was habit.

"Go ahead," Lucid said. "Check it."

It was difficult at times to tell whether he was being backhanded with a comment like that, as he often had a flat, emotionless manner of speech. Until he was upset. He was likely honest about wanting her to check the message, but his tone also telegraphed it bothered him.

She would wait. Jacob wanted to make plans to go out, and she kept having other things to do. Between her erratic work schedule at Consumia's Spiritual Emporium (a mixture of days and nights throughout her five days), household stuff (although Lucid wasn't messy—he was a neat freak—he wasn't paying bills, washing clothes, food shopping, or cooking much, either), and generally taking care of Lucid, she had little to no personal life. The Emporium was where she mostly interacted with others.

Raine placed her hand near the small of Lucid's back (but not touching him) and edged him toward his bedroom. Like he was a young child somehow eight inches taller than she was. His egg-bed, lid open, rested a couple feet from the wall, almost in the center of the room. It needed that extra distance for the top to stay propped open. He'd had it a little over a month, since his twenty-first birthday, and she knew it soothed him. He sat on the edge of the mattress, leaning forward.

The bed was built by Linden Vowel, whom Raine knew from work at Consumia's Spiritual Emporium. It was made of naked, unvarnished wood, and rather than being perfectly rounded, was shaped more like an escape capsule from a spaceship. Decoration on the external shell wasn't important to Lucid. Word-invaded dreams often morphed into nightmares, which was why he'd modified the gifted egg-bed with a plastic fan near his head that blew down his body, pushing errant words out a wire-mesh vent at his feet. So he was well-ventilated, too. No stuffy coffin atmosphere. And he claimed the fan's white noise helped drown out catcalls from words. He'd installed stickered LED lights inside the egg so he could read in bed.

For his entire life, Lucid had said he wished he could live in an egg, shutting out all stimuli and living in a state of unending potential. Before Dad had commissioned the egg-bed as a present, Lucid had built something akin to a low-roofed tent above his bed. Rather than there being, say, three feet of space above him, it was only about eighteen inches; just enough room to slide in and roll over, allowing him to sleep in the equivalent of opaque mosquito netting. Like a tented cocoon. The purpose of the sheets was to deflect random words from hitting him and influencing his dreams. Every morning, he'd say he'd been reborn. Raine would say he was slowly morphing into an adult version of himself.

Otherwise, his room wasn't much different from a routine college student's: vinyl albums and a record player, books on shelves. Blackout curtains. A lava lamp that changed colors. A video gaming chair. Except there was the egg-bed. As far as Raine knew, he was the only person in the world who had one.

"What happened?" Raine said.

"Luc! It was Luc! You said you wouldn't tell people about eggs anymore!"

This was a lot for him, and she knew the words he was saying were being nabbed from the air around him. That's why some people said we only had so many words we could use in a day, and then the reservoir ran dry, but that wasn't really true. It wasn't like that. The problem was that it took energy to (even unknowingly) catch them, and over time we tired. Unchosen words continued to pummel us even after we quit trying to catch any. Sometimes the words overtook us and caused us to sink into our navel-gazing selves, making us dwell on things or leading us to distraction, or challenging and influencing our reactions. They could affect our dreams. Hence, Lucid needed a protective egg-bed. It was a thoughtful gift purchased by an otherwise relatively unthoughtful dad.

"Do you want to lie down on the floor?" Raine said. They hadn't done that in a long time. When they'd fought as children, what had begun as violence, the wrestling and pinning, had evolved into Raine holding Lucid still as a form of sympathetic kindness. Most effective, they'd learned, was for him to lie on his stomach with his head sandwiched between two pillows, and for Raine to lie on top of him watching cartoons. They called it a "headcheese sandwich." It usually didn't take long for him to feel better. He didn't overheat. Sometimes he fell asleep like that. She was much tinier than him now, but it would work if he wanted her to do it.

She was about to touch his arm, but stopped herself. "Did he loft them at you?" she said.

"No!" He told her about squeezing the egg, the breakage, and Lucador wiping it in his hair. He was getting more animated. "Too much egg! Too many words!"

He closed his eyes and lightly tugged at his hair, as if primping in front of a mirror. It was poking in more directions now as he played with it. He never wore hair product, but he'd tug and pull it until it was just right. And "just right" was not verified in a mirror. It was by feel. He based the timing of his haircuts by closing his eyes and feeling his hair. He said if gravity was winning the argument with the words around him, then he needed a cut. People probably assumed this was an intentional hairstyle, but he was just busying his mind, treating himself like a human stress ball. Maybe the spikes were protective.

"Mutables were flelling everywhere," he said. "They were taunting me, daring me to say them. But I couldn't. Those guys don't even know how much I helped them, and I can never tell!"

"You mean you didn't want to tell Lucador and Kick what you were going through?"

No response, but she knew this was what he meant. It was a curse. Lucid had been protecting them. Sometimes he took the side of flelling words, like when people were unintentionally, unknowingly damaging them.

"Did Luc apologize?" she finally said, softly. "For breaking the egg?"

"No." He sat silent again. Was he holding back a smile? He was squeezing his eyes, fighting back a bursting emotion. This couldn't possibly be a joke. She was ready to kill him.

"He hired me," he said, covering his mouth with the back of a hand.

"Hired you?"

"On the spot." He focused in a middle distance as he spoke. "I saw words like 'clean,' 'mess,' 'broken,' 'death,' and 'hope,' so I knew it was right."

"You saw the word 'hope' after Lucador broke an egg in your hand?"

"It surprised me, too."

His first real job.

"Well, that's wonderful!" Raine was legitimately happy for him. "The universe takes care of her own. When do you start?"

"My first lesson was cleaning up the broken egg."

FOUR

4. WILLIAM

"William, it's Geta," Geta said on his cell. She was William's ex-wife and the mother of Raine and Lucid. He knew who it was from caller I.D., but she always said her name anyway. "Are you still at the office?"

"It's only eight," William said, his voice cracking, cutting in and out like a poor phone connection. "And let me guess, today's the first."

"Are you losing your voice?" Geta had always accused him of being a hypochondriac.

"It's just a head thing."

"But I bet you still played golf this morning."

Of course he had. She was just trying to needle him and he wasn't going to bite. But he didn't need his voice swinging back and forth like a golf club, either.

"It's already Monday and you know damn well that the first was Friday," she said. "That's when their rent's due. You're supposed to pay me the last day of every month."

She was talking about the kids' rent again. This was a monthly routine. Raine worked at Consumia's Spiritual Emporium and Lucid didn't work at all. Maybe Raine could afford a small place on her own, a studio apartment, perhaps. More likely she would need a working roommate with whom she could split rent on a two-bedroom, rather than living with an unemployed brother who stayed home reading or playing video games. But Raine was enthusiastic about taking care of Lucid. She loved him and they seemed to communicate well.

So yeah, it made sense for William and Geta to cover the kids' rent. They'd decided this was a better situation than Lucid staying on with either parent, who were enjoying empty nesting—William with his long hours at work and Geta traveling with some new guy he hadn't met yet. William was envious of the fun those two were having; the reports coming from Geta were one-sided, of course, but he thought about how often he'd traveled alone for business back when they were still married. She'd stayed home with the kids while he played golf. It was work, but it was still golf, too. This was now Geta's time to see the world.

Geta hadn't fought him about alimony. Attorneys for both sides plugged in the standard rate in California and she kept the house. He kept the summer home. He only paid for one year of child support for Lucid, since Raine was over eighteen by the time the divorce was finalized. No custody battle either, but William agreed to pay the lion's share of the kids' rent.

"All right. I'll send money," William said. "A call from the family means it's time for a check. They'd get it in my will, anyway, so they may as well receive it now."

"For fuck's sake, William, it's digital. It'll take you ten seconds. Why don't you set up autopay?"

"I'm not auto-paying. I prefer to make people get on the horn with me."

"No one's stopping you from calling the kids."

"All I am is a check to my family."

"Too bad the family couldn't keep *you* in check." They often spoke like this. Two slightly different conversations at once, and she was quick-witted, one of the initial things that had attracted him to her.

"I take it I'll see you at the party this week," William said, voice steadier, but still resigned.

"I haven't decided yet. And I'm sure you'll be sick." There was a moment of silence. Geta, Raine, and Lucid were all good at employing silence as a weapon. It provided more room for him to make an ass of himself. He didn't bite. "Now call the kids," she said.

They hung up.

WILLIAM TOOK a sip of water from a mug branded by Progressio, an Omniscian from CSE. Things like "progress," "caffeine," "motivation," and "wake up" were screen-printed along its surface in a scattered fashion, and he imagined this was how flelling words might look to Lucid. The coffee was a liquid version of a Progressio Lodge—or was it that Progressio was a human iteration of caffeine? Either way.

The party he'd mentioned to Geta was for William's mother, who was turning seventy-five on his parents' fiftieth wedding anniversary. Yes, his father Lewis had married Marian on her twenty-fifth birthday. If only William had been as smart. He'd just forgotten his wife Olivia's birthday last month. The somewhat submissive little waif didn't speak to him for three days, until he'd deduced what the problem was. He later figured each day had cost him another two hundred and fifty dollars in gift value. He'd never be as passive-aggressive as she was, whether with work or family. She should've told him what the problem was, so he could own up to it and make things better. He did, anyway, but it'd cost him. And leaving him guessing had driven him crazy. He should've married Olivia on her birthday. That, there, was proof of his dad's genius.

~

HIS OFFICE LINE RANG. It was Phil. He was only, what, fifty feet away?

Apparently, one of their bigger clients was being audited, triggered by the client's soon-to-be ex-wife. There may be some shady dealings causing red flags they needed to sort through. Not a job for a junior accountant; Phil wanted William on this one. With the complicated businesses and tax shelters the client had set up, some still in progress, this would take months and likely lead to a court appearance. The forecast called for heavy workloads with scattered book-cleanings.

Just what he needed.

After he and Phil hung up, William submitted the digital payment to Geta from the app on his phone. She'd been known to make him transfer money while still talking to him, to watch it happen in real time. "No check's-in-the-mail bullshit," she'd say.

Before the phone's screen had even gone back into sleep mode, it rang again. It seemed everybody was trying to get a hold of him today.

"Greetings, Dad," Lucid said.

"Lucid," William said.

Silence. This would be uncomfortable with anyone else. Sometimes Lucid only needed to hear William's ambient noises, just to know he was there. But Lucid never called for small talk, either, and William appreciated that.

"I'm well," Lucid finally said, as if William had asked.

"Ditto."

"If you saw me now, you'd see the words 'hired,' 'employee,' 'workforce,' 'economy.'" Despite Lucid's relative monotone, William could hear the excitement in his voice.

"That's great, Lucid. Who hired you?"

"Luc and Kick." These names didn't ring an immediate bell. "At Omnist II."

That meant he'd be working for the same lady as Raine was —Connie of Consumia's Spiritual Emporium. Lucid and Raine lived close enough to walk to the Omnist II location, so Lucid wouldn't need the metro line or a ride share for his commute.

After about a hundred-word description of the job, Lucid changed gears. "Are you sick, Dad?"

"I'm okay." William wasn't lying. "Okay" was a relative term, subject to your current circumstances. He felt poor for a living person, but okay for being dead.

"You sound like words have been attacking you. You need an egg, too."

"I've thought about that." He'd be sleeping eternally in a casket-shaped egg soon enough.

"I like to sweep the apartment of loose words before I go to sleep," Lucid said. "Get rid of the ones that don't belong. You should do that tonight."

"Sounds like a good idea," William said. "Now get some rest. You got a big day tomorrow."

"Night, good," Lucid said.

"Night, good."

Lucid had been surprisingly loquacious. A hundred and fifty words from him was equivalent to a thousand from Raine.

He wasn't going to assume Lucid could keep this job, much less make enough money to wean himself off the financial teat. But when word got out William had died, Lucid would get some inheritance right away. Then he'd get a second round when he turned twenty-five.

William knew the original CSE location in North Hollywood fairly well. After Raine had been hired a few years ago, he'd visited the store a few times, and after attending a Progressio Lodge, he subscribed to the Omnist and began receiving Motes: notifications that consisted of suggestions, advice, quotes, and occasional product pushes.

He received one presently.

MOTE:

No child should die before their parents.

LUCID. William worried about his son's wellbeing. Like, what would happen if Lucid insisted on living alone? Or if Raine got married? Now that Lucid had his first real job that wasn't just collecting balls at the golf course for a few hours while William played a round, William uncovered a new set of worries. Lucid used to miss a lot of school due to agoraphobia or hypochondria or something. Would he now miss too much work? Would there be inherent danger in the new job? How would he deal with customers and coworkers?

Lucid's call, followed by the Mote, was too coincidental not to be taken seriously. Sometimes the Omnist knew. William wouldn't admit it to anybody at work, but the Omnist had helped him a great deal post-divorce.

Maybe the Mote was about him, not Lucid. William had already died before his parents.

But he worried about Lucid, too.

CHAPTER
FIVE

5. RAINE

Two days later, on her way to work at Consumia's Spiritual Emporium, not even off her block yet in Echo Park, Raine slammed on her brakes to avoid hitting a ginger dog being chased by a young blonde girl. The child could've been Raine thirteen years ago. The dog could've been Shooby.

As a child, Lucid had always told Raine he wanted a cat, as cats were loners who could hide away in enclosed spaces, but their father was allergic and wouldn't allow it. As a compromise, the family went to a shelter to pick out a dog, and Lucid was instantly attracted to only one. She had orange, medium-length hair, floppy ears, and made the most eye contact of all

33

the dogs. Lucid said words like "peace" and "friend" were flelling about her. She was believed by the staff to be a spaniel and beagle mix, and they'd named her Sparkle.

"Her name is Shooby," Lucid had said.

"It's only fitting Lucid names her," Mom said, "since he couldn't get a cat."

"I didn't name her," Lucid said, pointing at the air above Shooby. "That's her word."

That flelling word was what he would later call an Obdurational, which were mostly nouns that didn't venture far from their objects, tethered and inseparable. A change of mood or scenery didn't affect an Obdurational. Interestingly, as far as Raine knew, "Shooby" was the only name she'd heard Lucid notice above a person or animal.

Raine felt close to Shooby, as she did with all life, really, alive or dead, communicating without words to any soul that happened to pass by, so naturally, a family dog with her cluster of feelings was a source of connection. The two were more than friends, more than family. And as much as she felt affinity for the dog, it was Lucid who was closest to her.

This was because Raine didn't need Shooby's affection and calming presence as much as he did. Lucid said that Shooby, just like him, could see flelling words and unique colors, and that he was the only person in the world who understood this about her. Shooby saw different words than Lucid did, of course, because she was a dog. For example, she had many more words for smells. More names for types of eye contact and tail positions. It was just a fact. And since Shooby was a happier creature, she saw more positive words than Lucid did.

They played a game where they seemingly ran in circles for no reason, saying they were chasing the word "ball" around the backyard. Or "squirrel." Or they hid behind trees and cars in the driveway from the word "seek." Raine didn't mind this, and would sometimes join in, not seeing the words, but being supportive. And it was fun. Mostly, though, she figured dogs liked chasing people who were running around, whether there were words present or not.

One day, they were all playing in the yard and Shooby snuck through their unlatched gate and darted into the street where she was hit by a car. Lucid was first to arrive, dropping to his knees next to her as the car sped away, the driver either not knowing or not caring that they'd hit a dog.

"She was chasing the word 'car,'" he said, crying to Raine when she caught up to him.

"Mom!" Raine called. "Dad! Come help!" She placed her hands softly on Shooby's heaving chest. Mom always said Raine could heal, that she could deliver heat and energy through her hands and give strength to another living being. Shooby needed this.

Mom was first to arrive, and she lowered herself next to them.

Shooby's fur was warm, but the backs of Raine's sweaty hands were cooled by the breeze. Shooby's chest didn't move for a couple seconds, then expanded and deflated quickly. A quick, painful-looking breath was followed by stillness for a second, then two, each breath taking longer than the last.

"'Pain,' 'sleep,' 'hurt,'" Lucid whispered. Then to Raine, "Are you healing her?" He dropped farther down so he and Shooby were cheek to cheek. Then he tried to lift her head and look in her eyes.

"Don't move her," Mom said. "I think she has broken ribs. Maybe more."

Shooby's eyes were closed as Lucid stroked the fur on her face. When he stopped petting and gasped, similar to the dog's irregular pattern of breathing, Shooby opened her eyes, staring straight ahead, catatonic. Lucid had worn that expression many times.

"It's working, Raine," Lucid said. "She's going to live."

Shooby closed her eyes again. The next breath took far too long.

"It's not your dominion," Mom said, standing up, petting Raine, who was petting Lucid, who was petting the doggie. As an adult, Raine was positive that that was what Mom had said, and it sounded so cold now. Removed. But at the time it seemed a natural thing to say, because ultimately, life and death weren't in their control.

Dad arrived at the scene.

"Shooby, Dad!" Lucid said. "Help her!"

People were gathering on the sidewalks of both sides of the street, and traffic had stopped in both directions.

"We should move her out of the road," Dad said.

Raine could feel Shooby had stopped breathing altogether. No spasms, no shaking.

Mom gently lifted Lucid by one arm. "She's dying, Lewis. Let Dad pick her up," she said. She rarely called him by his birth name. She was stern, but understanding. Sensitive, but distant. "The universe takes care of her own, and she had to call Shooby back."

"Open the back door of the car," Dad said to Raine while he slid his hands under Shooby's limp body. It was about a thirty-foot walk, and he carefully placed her in the back seat.

"Nooooo!!!" Lucid said as Mom drew him up the front lawn.

"I'm taking her to the vet," Dad said, closing the back door. He was moving deliberately, but not rushing. Raine knew Shooby was gone.

"I want to come!" Lucid said, fighting against Mom's grip on his arm.

"Come inside," Mom said.

Raine stood silently watching the car pull out of the driveway.

"Why didn't you heal her?" he said to Raine.

I did.

Lucid was inconsolable the rest of the evening. He wrapped himself in a blanket and sat on the couch, shaking and heaving despite the heat.

The next day, Raine found Lucid crying alone at a lunch table at school. Being alone wasn't the issue, as this was common for him, but that day he'd been picked on by other kids more abusively than usual. Flying, flelling insult attacks. Torpedoed words. Nowhere to hide. Which all exacerbated his crying.

She sat with him and used a textbook to bat away words she couldn't see flying at them. But she told everyone she could feel the incoming words, and that was all that mattered.

Lucid didn't eat, and spent the entirety of the lunch break hiding his face in his hands and making heartbreaking mewls.

That evening at dinner, Dad plied the kids for their versions of the bullying story, Dad claimed he had it all figured out. "I know what the problem is," he said. Then he paused, smug for a moment, waiting to be asked about it further. Whether it came or not seemed irrelevant.

"Forget about those other kids," Mom said. "They're just jealous."

Even Lucid wore a look of incredulity. Other students being jealous of Shooby dying in front of him was certainly not a thing.

"Geta, please," Dad said. "They're not jealous of you, Lucid. They just don't like you."

In some way, Raine found this a refreshing burst of painful paternal truth, but maybe its delivery was poorly timed. Lucid returned to his shell, saying nothing, stabbing at a piece of broccoli that kept bouncing off the tines of his fork.

"William!" Mom said, then changed her tone for Lucid. "They're jealous of your wonderful features."

"Whether or not they like him is pointless," Raine said. Even at nine years old, she spoke like this. "There's something wrong with them. Don't they know they're going to die, too?"

"Some people," Dad said, "they were damned before they were born, and will be damned when they die. They were granted brief respite to live a human life, a cigarette break from eternal damnation. What's a little extra sin? It won't matter one way or the other."

They never learned where Dad had taken Shooby. Not to the vet, not buried in the backyard. There'd been no mock funeral. They just never saw their dog again, and Dad always managed to dodge their questions about her. His distance and refusal to provide details made everything feel worse. All he would say was, "Shooby's a lucky dog. We're a lucky family."

Even when Dad was right, it felt like the worst thing ever.

As Raine walked up to the front door of CSE that afternoon, she had to navigate a sea of young Consumerians gathered out front. This was a big change from a year ago when the people who gathered there were picketers and protestors after a Consumerian, an Ornatuan named Javy, had died in the Dark Arts room following a Lodge. "Close down that scary satanic retail hub of murder and ghosts and all things horrific!" they'd said in so many words. These new fans were mostly local teenagers and, rather than screaming to shut it down, they wanted more Lodges, more stories and urban legends, and had developed identities that aligned with these things. The kids shared stories about Yksian and Ornatu, for example, Omniscians who seemed like gods to them.

Generally, these kids consumed artisanal sodas, kombuchas, Yksian's roasted garlic and pepper cricket Horror D'Oeuvres, and Lucador's Mexican cola-flavored beef jerky. It was like one had to partake in CSE's oddities as a rite of passage to join their club. Their soundtrack was a goth and punk playlist streaming from someone's phone. Those kids not wearing platform boots kicked around a CSE hacky sack.

As Raine parted the teenager sea, she slowed her walk to greet them. She knew most of them by name.

Lily was in the middle of a discussion with a couple of her friends. "You know that Javy was a musician, don't you? He had a magic guitar that conjured spirits from the other side."

"What are you talking about?" Juju said. "He was murdered by the spirit that was trapped in it. It tried to possess him."

"Raine, what do you think?" Lily said. She was wearing a T-shirt for the band The Color Braille, a dark electronic band Raine's coworker Kat probably listened to.

"I think if music isn't rescuing you from something, stop doing it," Raine said.

"But isn't it true all his tattoos came to life, killing him?" Juju said.

"I also think if tattoos aren't saving you," Raine said, "stop doing that, too."

"I heard the cat that hung out here last fall is really a were-cat," Gunnar said. "And that's why we don't see him anymore."

"Yeah, but he and his friends still come back for Lodges as people," Lily said.

"Sounds like you guys would enjoy Jasmine's Lodges," Raine said. "She's our resident pet psychic."

"But this stuff's real, right?" Gunnar said. "They're not just urban legends?"

"I'm not quite sure what an urban legend is," Raine said, her voice piquing with interest. "Strange things happen to those who look."

Gunnar turned to the other two. "The more she won't answer, the more you know she knows."

Raine curtseyed for the group and continued inside. Back when Javy's death was fresh news, Lucid had refused to step inside CSE for months. "It wasn't a curse and you know it," he'd said. "Javy was attacked by words. People who don't know, they call it a curse. Anyone can make words angry, even without trying, and then the words get even."

CHAPTER
SIX

6. LUCADOR

Lucador called the workshop in back of Omnist II the Forgery. It wasn't a huge space, nothing like Lucador had converted in his garage at home, but it allowed him to work on some of his projects at the store. He had a tabletop gas forge Kick insisted could only be used outside in the alley, and Lucador could forge knives, work on leather sheaths, decorate hilts. Forging swords would exclusively be done at home, still. The downside of the Forgery was that Kick and Lucid were in the main room, out of conversational reach. This drove Lucador crazy.

"I don't like the 'two' in the store's name," Lucador said when he entered the No-Basil Alcove, pretending to polish a hunting knife he'd engraved with his logo. "We're not a sequel. We should be a number one. Like 'Lucador's Pachyderm.' That's a great name." He sometimes called his followers his

Pachyderm at Lodges. Some Lucadorians repeated it in jest, but it hadn't really caught on.

"We're not 'two'; we're the second, as in royalty," Kick said. He was sitting at the register, his laptop open on the counter, waiting for a customer who was browsing a rack of Paula & Derby biodegradable sunglasses. "Are we going to talk about this every day?"

"HaHAA! That's it! I'm going by Lucador the First from now on. Watch how popular I get!" Kick wasn't biting. Sometimes Lucador could rile him up, sometimes not. "The Omnist is a good name for the app, not for the store."

"I like how the Omnist catches the words so I don't have to," Lucid chimed in, apparently catching a few. He was stocking cold items in the wall of refrigerator. They'd sold a lot of beverages at the Lodge last night. Kick had been right, the more spicy fruit tea they gave away, the more people bought expensive bottled beverages. Lucador hadn't initially believed Kick's math, but the price of one large bottle of kombucha paid for an entire cistern of free beverages.

And this Lucid kid, he knew how to talk, which meant *not too much*. That was the way children should do it. There were customers yesterday who spoke more in three minutes than Lucid did his entire shift. And even if his words weren't intended to be riddles, they sounded like it. Just like Raine. No wonder they were siblings.

"I like how Lucid talks in the short sentences," Lucador said. "Chopped up. Straight to the point." Lucador flipped his branded hunting knife in the air and caught it by the handle. One rotation, two rotations, then three. "Sometimes swords need to be chopped down into knives. Same with words. Same with salad."

"Word salad?" Kick said.

"Minced beef, pork, and chicken. Big minces. A little wine gravy poured on top. Now that's a good salad."

Lucid began breathing heavily, like he was mildly hyperventilating.

"Is something wrong, Lucid?" Kick said.

"Eggs?" Lucid said. He was looking at a box he'd just opened with twelve cartons of one-dozen organic eggs. A gross.

"Those don't need to be refrigerated," Kick said. "Only refrigerated eggs need to be refrigerated, if that makes sense."

"I thought you liked the eggs," Lucador said. The shells were uneven shades of brown, like lightly tanned leather. "And great for dipping in the colors. You like colors."

"We sell eggs?" Lucid said.

"We do now! That egg that met your hand, that was a sample. We won! HaHAA!"

"Don't worry about those," Kick said. "I'll put those out, if you want."

This seemed to calm Lucid down. He closed the lid on the box.

A FAMILIAR-LOOKING woman entered the store. All three males noticed her. Late twenties, olive skin, large dark eyes, and may have had recent ancestry from northern Africa or the Middle East.

This was the opportunity for Lucador to shine. He imagined himself a barbarian from an 80s movie, an old school hero in modern times. He also had no skill whatsoever at normal conversation, so his entire game was to make people notice him. He jumped in the air, landing with his legs spread and knees slightly bent. It was both an offensive and defensive stance. The ubiquitous stance. He held out his hand, both ready to pull and rescue, and to shake politely. "I forget the name," Lucador said. "Your name."

"Sydnee," she said, taking his hand.

"Hi, Sydnee," Kick said, waving, then returned his attention to his computer. Lucid was sitting on the floor counting and separating gemstones into groups of colors. Lucador was now alone in this journey.

"I am Lucador the First!" he said. As much as he wanted to, he didn't bow, but placed his other hand over his appendix as if about to.

"The First now, huh?" Sydnee said. "I don't remember you saying that at your Lodge."

"Ah yes, you're a Lucadorian, of course. I've seen you before. One of the many in the vast Pachyderm."

"Pachyderm?" Sydnee said. "I don't remember you saying that either. I'd rather not think of myself as a pig."

"No, no, not the pig. More like the elephant."

"You mean a memory."

"No, I do not forget. I have a great memory!"

"A herd of elephants is also called a memory."

"Interesting!" This was great news. "Lucadorians are a memory of pachyderms! Don't forget the memory! I like this! Thick skin. Smart! Like Lucid here."

Technically, he thought of Lucid as intelligent but thin-skinned, as someone who needed extra protection, a shell for safety. He wasn't quite Pachyderm material yet. But this moment now called for chivalry and gentlemanly manners in the presence of a lady. A memory lady.

Sydnee looked at Lucid, sitting cross-legged now with neat piles of rocks all around him. She studied him curiously.

"And you are Sydnee the First?" Lucador said, breaking her spell.

"Well, no, because that implies there's a second. And I have no children that I know of."

It took Lucador a moment, then, "HaHAA! A joke!" A woman not knowing if she'd had kids. He couldn't wait to tell Kick. "Did you hear?"

"I heard," Kick said, not looking up.

"So, I won't be a first," Sydnee said, nodding at Lucid. "Until there's a second in relation to me."

Lucador suddenly realized the implications of her statement. "Oh, the Lucid boy," he said. "Just an employee. But he does the tricks, so maybe we'll travel together. Like a carnival." Lucador smiled broadly. He'd been complimented many times on his wide mouthful of straight teeth. Yellowed from tequila and hand-rolled cigars, but straight.

"Oh, is he a gypsy?" Sydnee said.

"Not a gypsy boy, a carnival boy! Come see the marvel!"

Kick was staring. Lucid was staring. Even Lucador wasn't sure what he'd meant by that. He would figure it out later, if needed.

"Sydnee, can we help you with anything?" Kick said, still the farthest one away. His tone was even, but Lucador was sure it was a jab about Lucador's poor customer service skills.

"I'm looking for exorcism tools," she said. "I've already tried using a crucifix, Bible, and holy water."

"Sounds appropriate," Kick said.

"We don't have those anyway," Lucador said.

"Luc, do you think she'd come *here* if that's what she's looking for?" Kick said.

"I do have a pair of wonderful chakapas I got at CSE," Sydnee said.

Those are shamanic rattles! One step ahead!

"They're for when there's trouble out in the desert," she said. "I go to parties out near Indio, Joshua Tree, or Havasu and

45

sell merchandise for a few hours, then I pack up and join the dancing under the night sky. We welcome all the spirits to join us. The DJs know what to play, and the spirits sometimes take over and celebrate as corporeal entities, using our bodies. At sunrise, the spirits usually move on and we all collapse, spent and exhausted. But sometimes a spirit doesn't want to leave, making the host extremely sick, and I have to perform a ritual with the chakapas. If people see long trails of green, blue, or gold coming from them as I move, you know it's working, and the spirit moves on."

"Wow," Kick said. "I'd like to see that."

"We have the chakapas, too!" Lucador said. *Two can play the game of the Emporium!*

"Again, Luc," Kick said. "She said she already has those."

"I'm looking for other options," Sydnee said. "I tried the chakapas again this morning. Nothing."

"Ah, sí! Never to fear!" Lucador said. *I'll show Kick!* "Come with me!" He descended the aisles to present different items, like bundles of white sage, exorcism oil, and anti-ghost spray. He collected and handed them to Sydnee, who read the story card tied to the spray bottle.

"But it says not to spray people," she said. "Or breathe the fumes or get it on your skin."

"HaHAA! Like the bug spray!"

"But it's for exorcisms, right?"

"You spray the ghost!"

"I think it's missing the point here. I'll pass."

"Ah, sí. This is better! Take this!" He gave her a bottle of an O'Cult-branded herbal potion that warded off spirits, as well as a crystal the size of half a banana. "To heal the room after. Keep it free of the demons," he said.

"I have sage and many crystals already, thank you," Sydnee said. "But with these, I can rub on the exorcism oil, say my spell, then use this potion to keep the spirit from returning?"

"Demons begone!" Lucador announced. He was proud of his work. Kick must notice.

Kick rang Sydnee up, and after she left, the store felt empty. *This woman*, Lucador thought. *One of a kind*. Then he saw the lonely piles of stones on the floor.

"Hey, where is the Lucid?" Lucador said. He looked down each aisle, then walked into the Forgery, which was a messy mishmash of worktables and stacks of boxes and junk. "Lucid!" he called. He didn't see him and returned to the main room to report to Kick. "Not back there. Maybe he went to get cigarettes. Maybe he's getting a real beverage, a Mexican cola."

This was a running argument between them. Kick insisted many times your body didn't recognize any difference between corn syrup or cane sugar. But Lucador preferred using cane sugar cola in the marinade for his teriyaki-flavored beef jerky. Even though Kick said cola teriyaki didn't sound right on paper, he admitted it tasted pretty good in the jerky.

"Maybe you really pissed him off," Kick said.

"The egg thing in the hair, ancient history." Lucador waved it off, swords and knives jangling.

"It was only a couple days ago. And now we're carrying those same eggs."

Lucador followed Kick into the Forgery to look for the boy. Still no Lucid. Kick opened the fire door and looked up and down the alley. "Lucid!" he called. "Where are you?" He came back in.

"If I was a jittery little boy," Lucador said, "afraid of the eggs and the colors and people, where would I go?"

"Be nice, Luc. He might hear you."

"I'm not making the fun! He'll tell you the same!" Lucador said. "I'll find him. He's just hiding. Like in a jungle!"

Lucador lifted a swatch of canvas precariously strewn between his anvil and a shelf. He never covered his anvil. He found Lucid under a makeshift tent made from flattened boxes against the wall. A wall-mount for Lucador's chisels, tongs, punches, and hammers served as a buttress for the impromptu roof. The fort was barely large enough to contain a skinny, sprawling boy. Lucid had created his own cocoon within the Forgery.

"What are you doing back here?" Lucador said.

No response.

"Safe from the words!" Lucador said. Still nothing. "Anything to say?"

"Leave him alone, Luc," Kick said.

"Well?" Lucador rubbed the top of Lucid's head, no egg in his hand this time, as he cleared boxes out of the way with his other arm, destroying the makeshift shelter. "Soon you'll be too tall for Uncle Luc to rub your head, make the hackles."

Lucid was already an inch or two taller than Lucador, and not likely to grow any more. "Sometimes a soul's just hurting really bad," Lucid said.

"You know Lucador's just trying to help you, right?" Kick said.

"Not me, the lady," Lucid said. "Sydnee."

"She exorcises the demons!" Lucador said. "She's all set up now!"

"But maybe her person isn't possessed, but just struggling inside, panicking, realizing they're in the wrong egg."

"But she'll get them out of there! They'll go to the right egg!" Lucador said. "Or body. You know what I mean!"

"Raine can heal," Lucid said. "We found a bird dying on the ground. She cupped it in her hands and whispered it would get better, and I saw the word 'heal.' Then she opened her hands and the bird flew away. I bet she can fix Sydnee's person who's acting out."

Maybe she could. Lucador liked Raine.

Lucid walked back to the front of the store.

"Do me a favor," Kick said. "You hired him, so stop treating him like he's an eight-year-old."

"He ran away from home and we found him," Lucador said. "What else can we do?"

"It was the 'carnival boy' comment. Ease up on him."

Lucador slapped an arm on Kick's shoulder. "You like him, too," he said.

Everybody likes the Lucid.

CHAPTER
SEVEN

7. RAINE

Tonight's Lodge at Consumia's Spiritual Emporium was hosted by Nachie, an Omniscian whose focus was randomness. Despite the loose-sounding topic, his *Read-Animation* graphic novel series T-shirt, eyeglasses, and unassuming tone of voice revealed a curated and manicured sense of style. He was well-read and soft-spoken, with a confidence parlayed more by knowledge rather than a pedantic tone.

"Science tells us that nothing is random, that everything has a cause we can search for. God doesn't play dice with the universe, as they say. That's what science is, the study of cause and effect, so the mindset is to believe all effects have causes."

Raine both agreed and disagreed with this. Some things people just weren't meant to understand, although a desire and commitment to learn more was admirable. Internal soul-searching and external universe exploring were both natural instincts that should be nurtured. Even if answers weren't found, the new questions the search dug up were a type of answer.

Raine's phone lit up with a notification.

MOTE:

Life begat life; life feeds on life.

FOR THE FIRST couple years at CSE, Raine hadn't subscribed to the Omnist, and preferred sharing Omniscians' ideas in person. At Lodges. But about a year ago, after taking on new responsibilities that included writing Motes for various gods and generic Omnist advice and reminders, she had to join for quality control.

"But science also tells us some particles can be in two places at once, called superposition, until they collapse into one when observed," Nachie said. He slowly moved from one corner of the stage to the other. Like a gas in a container, or a bouncing ball screensaver, he covered every inch of it during a Lodge. "Or that a photon is both a particle and a wave until observed, the way you can consider a cat in a box to be both alive and dead until the lid's opened. You don't know which one it is beforehand, and there's no way to predict it. One form just takes hold when observation occurs. This all sounds pretty random to me. I think this is science's way of incorporating randomness into the theories while pretending it's not just a collective shrug."

The delivery of Motes could be considered random. Kick often bragged about how the ones he wrote were often produced by random word generators and bullshit artist websites. But then Consumerians found unique instances in their lives that the Motes applied to. And even though Raine's often sounded vague, like the one she just received, they still had a sense of precision to them. She wanted to inspire profundity through profundity.

All Motes were then filtered through the Omnist's algorithm and delivered to Consumerians who followed the gods and the Omniscians who belonged to them. In a way, Raine's precision inspired randomness, and Kick's randomness inspired precision. Motes in boxes; they were both random and precise, both dead and alive, until read by the users.

"The God of Randomness, Temerasus, wants you to worship all gods," Nachie said. His glasses implied he couldn't see clearly, but his expression said his vision was just fine. "Not all at once. Let him pick one today, another tomorrow." He golf-clapped for emphasis as he mock-counted. "Make a list, of five, ten, twenty gods, as many as you relate to, as you feel apply to you, and then roll the dice."

He rubbed his hands together, then opened them to reveal a set of three dice. Magic and non-magic, an illusion. But the dice were real.

"If you follow six gods, rolling a die will allow Temerasus to pick the one you need at that moment. Then read that god's thought of the day on the Omnist. Even if you think you know what you need, you may not."

Nachie walked to the edge of the stage and stopped in front of an Executive Saint Consumerian named Patrick. "Would you mind handing me the piece of paper in your breast pocket?"

Patrick looked around, confused. Everyone was looking at him. He was holding back a smile at first, which then broke wide as he found a folded piece of paper in his breast pocket.

"May I?" Nachie said, taking the paper from him. He unfolded it and showed it to the audience. "As you can see, I've written down a list of gods here, numbered one through six. And Temerasus is not one of them." He handed one of the dice to Patrick. "Will you roll for me? Just right here on the stage."

Patrick took the die and shook it in his hand. "Come on now! No craps! No craps!" he said, smiling. Several Consumerians laughed as he tossed it on the stage.

"Three!" Nachie said. He handed the paper back to Patrick. "Will you tell me what god that is?"

"These are the gods I follow!" Patrick said, looking at the sheet. "How did you—"

"Indeed. Now who is number three?"

"Salvu."

"Ah yes, the god of certainty, assuredness," Nachie said. "See? Temerasus, the God of Randomness is recommending Patrick heed Salvu's words today. Will you open the Omnist on your phone and click on Salvu's thought of the day?"

Patrick did as he was told.

"It says, 'Sometimes it's safer out in the open, out in the light. Be that light by apologizing for the misunderstanding you had with your father this morning.'"

"Pretty specific, right?" Nachie said.

"How did you—" Patrick looked back and forth between his phone and Nachie.

"I had nothing to do with that. That's why I don't care for horoscopes. Even if they're correct, they have to be vague enough to incorporate all the potential readers. When Temerasus is your guide, the God of Randomness will, oddly enough, individuate to you—the opposite of generality, using randomness to achieve a specific result."

〜

"Hey, Raine," Jacob Feynman said. He was a friend who'd asked her out several times recently to eat, or get a drink, or go to a show, and Raine was always busy. She wasn't avoiding him; she'd been legitimately tied up. He seemed neither awkward nor rehearsed. Not insecure nor overly confident. His eyebrows were naturally arched in an interested expression, like he was constantly taking everything in.

"I'd say it's random seeing you here," she said, "but I suppose nothing is random."

"Or everything is." Jacob said this like it was a good thing.

"I don't find it random that if you're writing your dissertation on theoretical mathematics you'd take in a Nachie Lodge."

"True, true," he said. He cleared his throat. He leaned over the counter to speak more quietly. "I don't know if you know, but Lost Maps is playing at Los Federales at midnight." They were a local jazz trio he'd talked about in the past. She'd never seen them. Raine appreciated a twenty-six-year-old USC grad student who enjoyed music not because other people his age liked it, or thought it was cool or of the moment, but because *he* liked it.

Tonight wasn't the best night, but then again, what night would be? Lucid had a job now. He was more independent than even three days ago. Maybe she could finally get away for a couple hours. Jacob may have been there for the Lodge, but he also wanted to see some music.

"I think tonight is a fine night for jazz," Raine said.

After the last customer left, Raine turned the "Open" sign around and told Jacob he could remain in the store as she performed her closing duties. Rather than play with his phone like everyone else their age, he strolled the aisles inspecting random items and reading story cards.

Raine texted Lucid:

Catching a show with a friend after work, I'll be home late. What are you doing?

~

LOS FEDERALES WAS ONLY a couple blocks away, an easy walk. The main level was set up as two rooms with two bars. The front bar was quieter than the back. Lost Maps had already begun playing, and their music grew louder as Raine and Jacob walked the length of the building to the back room.

The crowd was a mixture of young and old, and various races and genders. Dressed-up business types and dressed-down record enthusiasts. The Emporium was known for attracting all types, but the tide varied wildly by the Omniscian who performed each night. She supposed Los Federales was like that, too, but Lost Maps fans represented a good cross section of people.

The tables were all taken, but they found a single stool at the bar. Raine ordered a seltzer with lime and Jacob had a craft beer. Raine sat and Jacob stood, facing the band. The female drummer and male pianist were young, in their early twenties. The saxophonist was old enough to be their dad. His tone was soulful. Soft and breathy, which then built to a wailing, screeching, passionate crescendo.

"Do you hear colors when you hear music?" Raine said when the song ended. The saxophonist wiped down his instrument, while the pianist sorted some papers.

"I do," Jacob said. "Blue is one of the most common colors associated with jazz."

Lucid had told her once: "Unlike the common misconception, jazz isn't always blue, although it often is. To me, it's like an old, rusty tin with red and blue notes." To her, this description sounded like an old depression-era soda sign. "And mid to light brown is my least favorite color found in music."

"Do you see words?" Raine asked Jacob.

"I don't, but Lucid does, right?" Jacob said. He covered his hand over his beverage like he was embarrassed of it.

"The way Lucid describes it, musical notes are words, but they're also colors. Colored words."

"For me, the best music creates moods without need for words. With classical music, the strings and flutes invoke the sounds of angels singing. Jazz, on the other hand, is about people down here. It's earthier and human. The saxophone replaces the human voice." He lifted his hand off his drink to gesture toward the band. "This guy's good."

Raine had been listening through Lucid's filters. It was like he was sitting with them, pointing out highlights. "Music's math, too," Raine said. "But I'd rather hear colors than see numbers."

Jacob watched the musicians for a moment, standing completely still. "I find mathematics to be quite spiritual," he said. "Not like numerology, but in the structure of how the universe works. I've heard people argue about which existed first: matter or energy. I believe math existed before both. It's the skeleton that holds up the flesh of everything else, including music."

WHEN JACOB WENT to the restroom, Raine thought about how rarely she did this. Got out. She was basically a second mother to Lucid. Mom had spent eighteen years ignoring herself to raise him, with some help from Raine, of course, and Raine figured she'd help out a few more years. It was now going on almost three years.

Jacob was nice. Thoughtful, provocative, and not creepy. He engaged her when they spoke. He actually said something, even if they were just talking about the weather. He was smart. When he asked about Lucid, he wasn't just being polite.

She shouldn't feel guilty for being out with a friend after work, but she did.

Lucid hadn't responded to the earlier text yet. She texted him again:

Are you okay?

~

WHEN SHE AND Lucid had first started living together, Raine had gone on a date with a girl she met at the flea market, and she came home to find Lucid in the bath, door wide open, the water gone cold, reaching out at the air, like he was picking cherries off a tree. He was picking words.

There was a jazz station playing, the device resting precariously on the edge of the bathtub. He'd been a mere 3.1 magnitude tremor away from dying.

It's not like Lucid wasn't as smart as other people; if anything, he was smarter. But he seemed to think he was invincible. A clock radio falling in the bathtub was something that only happened in movies and books.

"Lucid!" Raine said. "Are you in a hurry to learn about the afterlife?"

"Don't worry, the cord's not long enough. If it falls, it'll unplug." When he stood, unashamed of his nakedness in front of her, he attempted to grab it to show her. She just barely got to it before he did.

~

WHY WASN'T Lucid responding to her texts now, though? This wasn't normal.

Jacob was walking toward her, returning from the restroom. She liked his gait. Not chest and muscles first, or leaning forward, headfirst. Not hips first. No ego, but not hiding either. Even. Steady.

"The witching hour bewitches," Raine said, as he slid his arm behind her, both to fit between stools, and to pick up his drink. "I must go home."

He looked surprised to hear the change of direction, but settled quickly. He took a last sip of beer. It was still half-full. He made a check-signing gesture at the bartender.

"You're doing so great, Raine," he said. Rather than argue, or complain that the set wasn't over, he'd complimented her. "I know getting out isn't easy. Thank you for coming."

"You can stay," she said. "My car's right down the street."

"I'm glad we're here, but I don't need to be in a bar with you. It's a proxy for anywhere, and anywhere is fine."

"And 'anywhere' has indeed been here."

Jacob walked her to her car, which was barely closer to CSE than Los Federales, and gave her a hug. She was happy to have spent some time with him, even if it hadn't been much. He may have understood, maybe not. He seemed to. Maybe she didn't need to date, yet.

After a crowded Lodge, followed by a bar full of loud music, she welcomed the silence of the drive home.

EIGHT

8. WILLIAM

Two nights earlier: Monday night:

William lay feet up, arms behind his head on his black leather couch, a piece of furniture he'd always wanted when he'd been married to Geta, but that she wouldn't allow him to get. "They're bad for kids," she'd said. "Plus, they're for bachelors. Are you still single in that head of yours?"

No. He didn't cheat on either of his wives like Phil did with his wife. He knew of at least three times Phil had been unfaithful, and those were just the instances William heard about. And if making money, playing golf, drinking scotch, and relaxing on a leather couch made William a bachelor, then so be it.

After living in a furnished apartment for a couple years, buying a house when he married Olivia meant he finally got to purchase his couch. He'd bought two of them. Now, though, he understood why they weren't a great idea. Even though the air conditioner was running, and he didn't feel warm, his back was sweating. He wanted to scratch it, but he couldn't reach. Decomposing flesh might itch; he hadn't thought of that. He lifted his back off the couch an inch or so and tugged down on his shirt to temporarily separate it from his skin. That helped a little.

He'd drunk some water today, after playing golf and a little at the office, but he still wasn't hungry. Water made sense. He didn't want to turn into a piece of leather, or crack and peel, while he was still animate. He'd been replacing what was evaporating. Maybe he should lotion up to last a little longer. Southern California was dry. He wished they had a humidifier in the house; he'd had one when he lived with Geta.

He hadn't needed the restroom. Dead people didn't go to the bathroom.

Olivia came over, lightly tapping his leg to get him to move back a couple inches, and sat on the edge in the middle of the couch. She stared at him. She didn't talk much. She didn't need to. She looked concerned. He'd learned a while back she could communicate better with her eyes, micro-gestures, and posture than anyone he'd ever met. It didn't mean William liked it, though. He didn't need to play guessing games. *If you're unhappy, say you're unhappy.*

"I don't know what I did that was so wrong," Olivia said.

She thought he was the one playing a game. This wasn't a game. It wasn't. But it felt good to shut down for once, to not have to make eye contact. It took less effort this way, and his energy levels had been volleying all over the place.

"First," she said, "you went to bed early last night, which is fine, but you wouldn't talk to me or eat breakfast this morning. And you couldn't wait to get out the door."

True. Those things happened. But I died.

He'd meant it earlier when he said he felt thankful. He may not have been openly happy, but he wasn't unhappy. He was thankful for financial stability. For having a wife eight years the junior of his ex-wife. For improving his game until he was nearly a scratch golfer. For having good kids who were living on their own. And Lucid had a job now, something he wouldn't have learned today if death had only turned out to be a black, dreamless sleep last night. So he was thankful for that, too.

"You said you'd talk when you came home, and you didn't come home until after ten o'clock." Olivia's tone was small and measured. She was afraid of him. At least she was finally saying what bothered her. "You were gone over fifteen hours. You still won't eat. Where were you? Did you go to dinner?"

I don't need to eat. I'm dead. I talked to my business partner, my ex-wife, and my son, but couldn't tell them I loved them. I sent Geta money for the kids' rent, so that means I'm still alive to her. I have a purpose.

"You're wearing too much cologne," Olivia said. "Were you on a date?"

A date with death.

"What's that supposed to mean?" she said.

I said that out loud? "Nothing. I played golf today and thought I could smell myself."

Geta would've turned the date-with-death comment into a burn. *If you'd rather fuck a corpse,* or something else off the cuff. Sometimes she'd cut him down so hard there'd be silence, as maybe she'd thought she went too far. Then they'd both start laughing. A good burn was a good burn, and he'd have to give it to her. Many of their arguments had ended that way. In laughter.

Olivia wasn't his soulmate. She was kind, quiet, sweet, pleasant, subservient, and took care of house and home. Cooked, cleaned. No kids. Her complaints were mostly centered around not spending as much time with him as she wanted. He'd heard that before. It was a refrain. If he'd met Olivia first, they would've made the prototypical nuclear family. She checked all the boxes he thought he wanted in a wife, until he saw he'd been using the wrong form.

Geta was his soulmate, but he'd blown that. She didn't put up with his shit. She was his equal and they were partners, except he'd turned and made himself partners with Phil, instead. That cliché about being married to your work? It was real. And it paid really well.

But he'd also lost Geta.

When Geta had been on the phone with him earlier, she could hear something was wrong with him. Maybe she didn't know he was dead, but her radar had been up.

"What's wrong?" Olivia currently said.

Can't you tell? If Geta were here right now, she'd know. He looked at his phone.

MOTE:

If you have no one to ask, is it really a question?

HE GOT up and went into the bathroom.

"William?" Olivia said from outside the door. "Was that from your girlfriend?"

The decorative soaps near the sink mocked him. He'd used one once and Olivia quietly lost her mind. *Don't put soaps or towels near a sink if they aren't supposed to be used.* He eyed the non-decorative hand towel he would use. Deciding early.

He sat down.

Should he tell Olivia or not? She was coming out of her shell like he wanted. Maybe it took him dying for this to happen. But she would try to convince him to get help. *Think, William, think.* He wasn't going to go to the hospital. Even if they didn't send him to the morgue immediately, they'd keep him overnight, or forever, in a bed. He may have to go in a bedpan, not in his own toilet, like he was right now.

Dead people didn't go to the bathroom.

WILLIAM HAD COME HOME from work after ten o'clock again. He still hadn't said anything to Olivia about what had happened to him the other day. Years ago, a psychologist told him it was called Cotard's syndrome, or Cotard's delusion. It's a condition where a person feels they're dead. Not while dreaming, but in everyday life. He'd slept off the rest of the episode Monday night, then silently ate breakfast with her Tuesday morning. He'd almost brought up the topic, but didn't.

It was Wednesday night now, and he felt alive. Not alive in the sense of taking the world by the horns, but he could feel his bodily processes working. He could feel his breath, heart, hunger, and digestion. Burying himself in work had been helping somewhat.

"I should go to bed," William said. "I'll need to put in extra hours tomorrow if I want to leave early for the party on Friday."

"Oh, are we talking today?" Olivia said.

He deserved that. "Just saying I should get some sleep."

"I wish you'd tell me what's going on," Olivia said. "Is there someone else?"

There's always been someone else.

"You act like you're so complex, like I wouldn't understand, but really, you're not," Olivia said. "We all have the same needs. It's okay. We have a roof over our heads, food on the table, someone right next to us who understands."

No one understood. He really thought he'd died this last time. The weird part was even though he could remember previous episodes while he was having a new one, he always thought things like, "This is the one. This one is real. This is so much realer than the other times. Those were all part of my condition. Now I really know what it's like to die. And everybody dies. We got to go sometime. This is it."

Geta had always taken charge when he had an episode, calling in sick for him, sticking a movie in front of him, but he couldn't tell that to Olivia. It would ruin her. For once, he was with someone who saw him the way he wanted to be seen. A leader. Strong. Decisive. And if keeping his secret meant she thought of him as a bit of an asshole, then that was preferred to her learning about his weakness, his instability. He'd rather be considered brooding and mysterious, and difficult to please.

"Did you hear me?" she said. "You understand me, don't you? I understand your needs." She stroked the back of his neck. "Now come to bed."

CHAPTER
NINE

9. RAINE

Walking in the door after Los Federales, Raine found the television had been taken off the wall in the living room and was lying on its face on the floor, with its guts and screws and circuit boards spread out like an autopsy scene.

Raine stepped over and around the mess and tapped on Lucid's door. "Lucid?"

No response. She tried the knob. It was locked.

She knocked again. "You're okay, right?"

She heard shuffling, and Lucid finally opened the door. "I told you to go away," he said.

"I'm sorry, I was unaware you said that."

"You always say that, too." He wiggled a finger in his ear. "You knock so loud," he said. He looked like hell. There were dark circles about his eyes, and the whites were bloodshot like he'd been crying.

"What's with the disembowelment scene out here?" Raine turned sideways, as if they could see the living room from his bedroom door. They couldn't.

"Here," he said, retrieving his phone from his charger to show her a Mote.

MOTE:

Fomotalia says go to bed.

FOMOTALIA WAS the goddess of FOMO, who spoke about the fear of missing out.

"I followed her advice, as instructed," Lucid said. He was definitely acting strange, even for him.

"You're too gentle a soul for the Omnist," Raine said. "You should delete it."

"I'm a man now. Being twenty-one means I'm independent. Lucador and Kick said having a real job means I can do anything anyone else can do. Like go get a drink if I want." But, like her, he wasn't a drinker. "So, after work, I went for a walk and bought some gummies."

"THC?" Raine tried to regulate her voice to avoid sounding hyperbolic, but she felt it come out her eyebrows. She lowered them. "Lucid."

"It was beautiful inside the shop: the black lights, the glowing counters, all the wonderful names for strains. Have you heard what they come up with for them?"

"I can only imagine."

"It didn't matter though, because of all the flelling. That's where the best words are, anyway. Words like 'relax,' 'think,' 'yummy,' and 'expansion' were everywhere. Expanding my mind is good, right?"

"I think, perhaps, that if there were ever an exception to that notion, you'd be it."

"The nice girl who worked there told me to try it at home first to see how I handle it. So, I came home and ate one."

"You ate a whole gummy? Why not just nibble a little first, to see if you like it?"

"But I did like it. I could've eaten a whole pack."

"Lucid." She felt the eyebrows again, but this time they were cinching.

"I was playing a record in my room, then my heart started racing. The word 'worry' jumped out of my chest. Right here. Along with 'panic,' 'stop,' 'slow.'"

"Oh, no."

"I couldn't calm down. I couldn't stop it. And I wasn't exercising or in public or anything." He took a deep breath. "I decided to draw the magic." He pointed at the pad on his desk in front of his computer. His sketchbook. "I had a vision of the colors I needed to draw. I used black charcoal. I could modify them by going lighter, harder, shading. Crosshatch. It was working, and yet it didn't work."

"Why didn't you just paint the colors?"

"You shouldn't have to cheat by wiping the exact color you want on the page. I thought you could change the frequencies of the light waves as you draw. Control them with your hand, with your mind. Then I rubbed my eyes, they were itching so much, and all the colors disappeared." That explained the dark circles. Charcoal. "Someone must've tricked me into getting stoned so they could watch me fail at making colors out of charcoal."

"Making colors out of black makes no sense," Raine said. "You see that now, right?"

"They must have still been watching and listening. So, I took apart the TV, looking for the listening device. I was sure if I found it, I could figure out who's behind all this."

"You mean another listening device besides the one that's already attached to the TV?" Raine said. "And besides the one in your pocket?"

"You're making fun. It's not in my pocket." He waved the phone in his hand at her. "And that's when Fomotalia told me to go to bed. I trust her. She knew I needed protection. Somebody had to protect our house."

Instead of being home and protecting Lucid, Raine had been listening to jazz in a bar. He wasn't blaming her, but she was feeling responsible. "But you know you're safe in here."

"I know. I locked my door and hid in my egg, but I realized my cranium was just another layer of shell, and when I went deeper inside, I found another shell. And another. It was regressive hell."

"Well, all the protective layers out here appear to be in good working condition. I checked. The lock to the building is working, the lock on the apartment door, all the windows and shades, the lock to your room, then the lid of your egg-bed."

"You haven't checked that one."

"I trust it's fine, Lucid."

"I couldn't even read. My mind was racing. I couldn't listen to music. The words and colors were coming at me too fast. I closed my eyes and it got worse. I could hear the blood flowing in my ears. I tried to focus on that. Eventually, I did math problems to calm down, assigning values to light frequencies and multiplying or dividing them to discover colors no one's seen before."

"It's like you could hear me talking earlier." At Los Federales with Jacob. He and Lucid had only met a couple times, when Jacob stopped by to pick her up, but she was sure listening to those two talk about colors and music and math would feel otherworldly.

"I discovered Sativalium."

"You mean sativum?"

"No, sativum's the Latin word it's derived from. Sativalium is the name of a relaxing color I found."

"The name suggests it's more of a substance than a color."

"Colors *are* substances." He was creasing his brow. "Just like numbers can exist outside the items they represent, colors can exist outside their objects, too."

"Numbers aren't substances, either." As soon as she said that, she knew she shouldn't have. She was tired. She never would've made that mistake in the morning.

Lucid sucked in a huge breath, looking fearfully at what she imagined were dozens of words attacking him. He pushed her uncoordinatedly to the hallway, then swung at something invisible above his head, blocking it from entering his room as he closed the door.

"Night, good," she said.

Raine returned to the living room and stood over the disassembled television, wondering what to do about it. A not-so-smart TV.

"Don't touch anything!" Lucid yelled from his room. He probably had to raise the egg lid in order to do this.

Guess she was leaving everything a mess tonight.

TEN

10. LUCADOR

He'd begun the day before dawn, as he always did, in the garage with the door open. The forge created concentric bubbles of warmth from the center of the room and pushed against the chill of the cold cement. The smell of hot metal battled with the cool breeze, and the sound of mourning doves reminded him where and when he was. He was often barefoot at home, depending on the task, since strong callouses on his feet represented strong callouses of the mind. Only exposure to elements properly prepared you to handle those elements. But for safety reasons he wore boots around his forge.

Lucador only needed about four and a half hours of sleep a night. Six hours was sleeping in. He'd get about four hours of work in before heading to Omnist II on his early shift days, and up to nine hours before his later shifts, like today. On his one day off from the shop, he taught sword-fighting classes in a local park. He preferred to do forge work before the sun heated the garage to uncomfortable levels. Then it was back inside to work on capes and vests and fingerless gloves. Precision work.

After coming home from Omnist II, Lucador would often focus on beef jerky or leather work. His bovinity. Last night, he'd stayed up late putting the finishing touches on a few sheaths.

He didn't use email, didn't have a cell phone, and didn't even have a laptop. He called people the old-fashioned way, on his landline. They could call him, too, but now that Omnist II had opened, he was home less during business hours and found himself almost exclusively calling his retailers to ask if they'd called him.

After an hour in the garage, a thought hit him.

"Sí, sí," he said to himself. "I know now, I know." And he decided to change up his routine today and skip ahead to the leather work. He found the specific cured pieces he needed and got to work branding, fashioning, and stitching. This was going to be a special item. The best of the best.

"HaHAA! VICTORY AT LAST!" Lucador said, walking in to Omnist II and seeing how Kick and Lucid had decorated the shop. It was set up for a Black and White Lodge tonight with the Omniscian Vogel Grey. "Just like I would do!"

They had taken black or white product samples, like Lucador's capes and Vogel's "magnetic" towels, and strategically covered the brightest of the colored items in the aisles or displays. Even the smart screens in the No-Basil Alcove were showing either all black or all white. The difference was striking. The store looked like a 3D chessboard, with multiple levels on the aisle shelves, counters, walls, and stage. The idea was to display as little color as possible.

"I like it, I like!" Lucador said. "Where is the Lucid?"

"I sent him home," Kick said. "He's dressing up for Vogel's Lodge, but he wants to surprise you by wearing one of your capes."

"This is good news! A good sign! The protégé impresses the mentor! Surprise me, then!"

~

LUCID ARRIVED with an even greater expression of unease than usual. He seemed to realize what he was wearing was nearly a Halloween costume, and it was five months until October. He was wearing black tights, a helmet, and white bandages wrapped around his chest and arms, with many ends hanging loose.

"Here he comes," Lucador said. "The warrior-mummy!"

"Army." Lucid touched the metal helmet on his head. "Garage sale. World War Two."

Lucador rapped on it with his knuckles. He appreciated the dull clank and the way it moved a little. "Safe brains. Keeps them safe."

"Nobody died in it, but the lady said it saved someone's life."

Kick surveyed the boy, the critical critic ready to criticize. "I'm not sure what look you're going for exactly."

"It's the black and white," Lucador said. He couldn't believe Kick didn't know this. "Except the helmet is the rugged army green. It's a good look!"

"Looks?" Lucid was distraught. "It's not about looks! It's

extra shell. The words are 'protect,' 'save,' and 'peace.' Not 'fashion,' 'image,' and 'costume.'"

"That's it, then! I figured it out!" Lucador said. "Extra shell makes you an egghead!"

Lucid didn't seem to enjoy the attempt at humor, exhibited by his wrinkled brow. But the helmet *was* army green, not eggshell white. Lucid should know this. He looked like a mummy who'd joined the army.

"Then the mum's the word!" Lucador said, trying humor again, pressing a finger to his lips.

Kick and Lucid stared for a few seconds. *They must be mumming.*

"If I were pressed," Kick said, "I'd say you're part soldier-ninja, part mummy-egg-man."

Lucid nodded, approving of this assessment. He lifted his leg with two hands to show them his foot. "Ninja shoes," he said.

Lucador had seen ninja shoes before, and these weren't them. These looked like something acrobats or gymnasts wore.

Raine had told Lucador that Lucid often wore a Soother-Wrap under his clothes to help calm him in public, which obviously now included going to work. Previously, these anxiety-decreasing undervests had been hidden out of sight, but here one was, black and partially exposed under white bandages. Lucador imagined it was tight on his torso to make him feel hugged and safe. Like the way Lucador's own girdle held him and protected him from backstabbing swordsmen. There was a public stigma against male girdles, but his theory was that the problem lay in the name. *Girdle.* Maybe something to bring up to Lucid the wordsmith later, away from Kick's prying ears.

"As humans, we all have a magnetic charge," Vogel said from the stage, holding a black and white checked towel. She was of indeterminate race. Her hair was a dyed black crew cut, but long in back, dyed white. A two-toned mullet. "Some people repel others, others attract. Some are positively charged, others are negative. Some are north, some south. Our blood, with its high iron content, attracts us to appropriate magnetic types."

She extolled the virtues of one of her branded magnetic towels, and how it affected moods with its pH balance and energy flow through the blood-brain barrier.

"The word 'attract' is flelling above Vogel,'" Lucid said. "That's how you know she's telling her truth."

"I do not see any words, young novillero," Lucador said. He was a bright boy, but maybe a bit imaginative.

"I see words around myself sometimes. Words like 'repel' and 'escape.'"

"That is good, then. Vogel's a good Omniscian for you. She is the north and you are the south. A magnet, a battery, a compass."

"Is she a moral compass, maybe?" a woman said right behind them.

"It's Sydnee!" Lucador said. The day continued to improve. "Lucadorians rejoice!"

"Hello, Lucador," Sydnee said. "Greetings, Lucid."

"Using north and south as descriptors implies a civil war," Lucid said, as if she'd been part of the previous conversation.

"No, there's no war here, Lucid." Sydnee was wearing a black and white checked hat. A white dress with long black gloves and black shoes. For as raggedy as Lucid looked as a black and white soldier mummy, Sydnee was a refined and elegant belladonna.

"Your flelling words," Lucid said, looking above her head and around her shoulders. "You have good ones."

"I'm sorry," Sydnee said. "'Flelling'?"

"It is a thing with the Lucid," Lucador said. "A game. No matter."

"How's it a game?" Sydnee said.

"It's not," Lucid said. "He just can't see them. Flelling is like flying, but words tend to stick close to their truths. Like, you have 'understanding,' 'teacher,' and 'inquisitive' about you. Those are great words."

"It's like an aura, then?"

"An aura of words, and words can have color, and color can be musical with notes and key, and key can..." Lucid seemed to lose steam, distracted by what Vogel was saying.

"Our understanding of colors is wrong," Vogel said. "Colors don't really exist; they're creations of our minds. Only frequencies of light waves exist, so therefore the color of everything exists on a continuum of intensity of light, and our minds invented the concept of color to match up with the frequencies."

Lucid was listening closely. Sydnee was looking at Lucid. Lucador wanted to be a good host and offer her something. Some beef jerky, maybe.

"Something can be both white and black," Vogel said, "but when chopped up fine enough, it appears grey to the eye." She held up another Vogel Grey towel. "But when you look closer, you'll find the black and white pixels are still there, sitting side by side. Grey is illusory. To deal with the contrast, out brain assigns it a consistent color."

"This is a good Omniscian!" Lucador said. "Finally, someone who gets it! Chop the colors down to individual parts!"

"It's not true," Lucid said. "It's not true."

Sydnee was watching Lucid more than Vogel, more than Lucador.

"And yes, I'm aware my last name is Grey," Vogel said. "It's my real name."

"I tried it, making colors with black charcoal," Lucid said to Sydnee. "It doesn't work."

"Our brains do this with sound as well," Vogel said. "What sounds like a continuous note is actually repeated waves or contusions of air hitting your eardrums. To process this and create value or meaning, our brains invent the concept of a consistent tone."

"Music has color, too," Lucid said. "It's real."

"I agree," Sydnee said, leaning toward him to speak quietly.

This is confusing. The boy doesn't like when strangers are close. But he is accepting her! What a woman!

"So, let's pray to the Goddess of Color, Vida Chroma," Vogel said. "For it is she who grants us the ability to fill our minds with all the wonderful colors of the rainbow."

"Excuse, me," Sydnee said, raising a hand and speaking up so Vogel could hear her from a distance.

"Yes?" Vogel said.

"Does Vida Chroma give music its color, then, as well?"

"Musical color? Like synesthesia? Why yes, she does. She grants color to all waves that need interpretation, and it is by her blessing we share in her gift."

"The ocean, it is waves, too!" Lucador said. Sydnee would surely know he was keeping up with the sciences.

"So, let's all close our eyes and pray," Vogel said.

Lucid was shaking his head, stepping backward, mumbling. "It's not true. Colors don't need us. Words don't need us. Or music. Nobody gives us these. It's their world and they let *us* live in it."

"The celebrations I go to," Sydnee said to Lucid, "they're full of music and colors. They dance and sing with us. The smells even have colors!"

"That's what I want!" Lucid said.

"We can talk about it later," Sydnee said.

"We welcome Vida Chroma into our hearts and minds..." Vogel said.

"Close your eyes, Lucid," Sydnee said. "Let's see the colors." She slipped her hand into his. She placed her other hand on him, as well, cradling his arm. *He's letting her touch him!*

Lucador didn't need this. He harrumphed and moved away to find Kick.

CHAPTER
ELEVEN

11. WILLIAM

Friday traffic was bad on the way to his parents' birthday-anniversary dinner. The get-out-of-towners were getting out of town. When the freeway was like this, the speed limit signs mocked him. Wouldn't you prefer to go sixty-five miles per hour? Good luck with that.

At a full stop on the freeway, he read a notification on his phone.

MOTE:
Even the dead have to wait.

SOMETIMES THE OMNIST KNEW. He wasn't just sitting in traffic at a dead stop, he was still feeling the aftereffects of thinking he'd died this week. This psychological hangover often lasted several days. He was burnt. Tired. In a way, death was like a vacation from life, and now he'd come back needing a vacation from his vacation. He would say nothing at dinner about the Mote. His children had experience with his mortal affliction, and he didn't want them worried about it. This most recent spell had been the first one since he and Olivia lived together. When he'd decided to marry her, he'd also vowed to keep more of his inner life private than he had with Geta. Olivia was a gentle person and a sweet wife who didn't have a dark side, so there was no need for her to be burdened with his curse. He was a man who could take care of himself.

Olivia sat next to him in the car, looking straight ahead with her knees together, hands clasped—a model of propriety. She always looked thoughtful, ready to understand. They hadn't spoken yet in the car, with her following his lead on not talking, and it wasn't until they arrived at the party that he finally said something.

"My lady," he said, nodding his head while opening the door to the restaurant. She almost looked fearful, the way she looked at him. He'd become scary to her. Maybe his tone of voice had been abrasive.

William's parents were seated at the bar awaiting everyone's arrival. Their faces lit up when they saw William, but even more so for Olivia. This didn't bother him; she needed to feel welcome.

He ordered himself a scotch, neat, and Olivia a glass of white wine. Golf highlights played on a nearby television. Good. He'd been so busy with business accounting forensics that he hadn't been updated on this weekend's tournament yet.

Dad was jolly as ever. Seemed British even without an accent. With a name like Lewis Oxford, he wore his heritage on his sleeve and could fake a dialect if he wanted. Great sense of humor. He had a wide-pored nose that bloomed red after his first drink, with its blossoming

matched only by his ears. He enjoyed old-fashioned drinks like Mint Juleps and Manhattans, but real men didn't need straws or toothpick umbrellas in their glasses.

William's mother Marian was the type who asked for special preparations with her food at restaurants. Or asked to be moved to a better table. Or to see a manager. She'd led her family for fifty years, and that wasn't about to stop because she was turning seventy-five. No drinking tonight for her, as her medication wouldn't allow it. It could cause a stroke, and she made sure everybody knew it, including the bartender.

"So, Olivia," Mom said. "Tell me about the house; what're you working on?"

This was good. Mom and Olivia could keep each other busy. House stuff was a safe topic. Olivia answered her question softly, drawing Mom closer.

"Oh, that's nice...wow...no, no, you go on..." Mom had all the phrases in her arsenal for entertaining guests and pulling them out of their shells. She mirrored gestures and repeated what her guests said, adding a verbal question mark, like, "The black one, you say?" and "All by yourself?"

Olivia had opened up a little, and the two women spoke with their stools turned toward each other at forty-five-degree angles, knees touching.

"Oh, that reminds me of when William was just a boy," Mom said. "He used to..."

William tuned them out. The women were drifting into dangerous territory, and he may become embarrassed if Mom told a story that he'd prefer be kept private. He attempted to converse with Dad about trimming the trees in the yard.

"Who needs a gardener when the lawn mower still works?"

Dad said. Here was an eighty-year-old man who could easily afford a gardener, but insisted on doing his own yardwork. First-world problems.

But Mom's conversation kept leaking into William's auditory field. She was telling a story about him as a boy hiding under a pile of coats in the closet. Embarrassing, but not that bad. He'd forgotten that one. *Just stay away from stories about death.*

"Say, William, when are those kids of yours going to arrive?" Dad said. That was his way of saying he was hungry.

"They both worked today, but they'll be here soon. Traffic. You know Lucid has an adult job now, right?" He was impressed with himself that he had a solid answer about the kids. They didn't talk often enough, but since Raine had declined the offer of a ride tonight, he knew this much, at least.

"You don't say," Dad said. "I'd always thought he'd get a job as a comma."

"Oh, Lewis," Mom said, overhearing, slapping his leg. "I told you about his job already."

"But why a comma?" William said.

"A *coma*," Mom said. "I'd told your dad the job would help Lucid step outside his comfort zone, and he said, 'What, out of his comma?'"

A play on words. A play on Lucid's flelling words, his emotional linguistics.

Sometimes William wished he had his dad's outlook on life. Not carefree by any means, but Lewis didn't get weighed down by the little things. He loved conversation. He loved people, life, and his family.

William, by comparison, loved his children in the sense that they were his progeny. He provided for them and kept them healthy, which allowed the genetic line to continue. Be strong. Lead by example. He'd named his son Lewis after his father, and hoped lots of the good-natured genes would pass down. But it turned out Lucid was nothing like his namesake. He was too reactive, too regressive. Keeping distance from others was fine, but he needed to learn when to step up and be assertive.

Raine, on the other hand; she was too philosophical, or ephemeral or something. Her feet never seemed to make contact with the ground. She spoke in quips and euphemisms. He hadn't seen her cry since she was a little girl, probably when she skinned her knee. It wasn't that she didn't have feelings, but she seemed to understand them in the way comedians understood humor. The best jokes didn't garner a laugh, but a "Now that's funny." By the time Raine was eight she was already saying things like, "I feel like crying." Before proceeding not to cry.

It could've been worse. The kids got along, and based on the way he'd heard his coworkers talk about their own kids, that alone showed he'd done something right.

And like Lucid, when William had an episode, he wanted to shut out the voices and noises of the outside world. But rather than hide himself under coats as an adult, William developed tunnel vision by focusing on work, bills, or other dry stuff Geta and the kids never seemed to think about. Logic and problem solving soothed him. So did putting. Practicing putting was useful on multiple levels: relaxation, escapism, tunnel vision, zen.

But tonight wasn't the time for salve. Families weren't logical and preferred listening to stories. A family wasn't merely a genetic line, but the stories of a group of related people: how couples met, how and where children were raised, how everyone got along. Stories about hometowns, hobbies, accomplishments, careers. Military service, diseases. Everything was anecdotal. Someone had to tell the stories. This was where William's dad shined.

∿

"Raine suggested me and Grandma come out to the Emporium for some sort of Coffin Club and decorate a couple of boxes," Dad said. "What do you think?"

That didn't surprise William. Raine often spoke fondly of the Coffin Club and its host, Linden Vowel.

"That's a bit dark," Mom said. "She's putting bad ideas in your head. Thinking about death all the time."

"Sounds pretty practical," William said, looking over at his wife. "Right, honey?"

Olivia nodded.

"She called them 'boxes,' though," Dad said. "Funny word for a coffin, but then again, maybe they thought calling it 'Box Club' didn't have the right ring to it." He laughed. "Maybe I could dance like a butterfly and sting like a bee."

More laughter. William was positive Olivia didn't catch the reference. "You see," William said to her. "That's a quote from a famous *boxer*. He used to say that."

Dad laughed again. Jolly Grandpa-Dad-Lewis was being jolly. "A coffin's a hell of an anniversary gift, eh William?"

That was a verbal jab that stung like a bee. William had forgotten to buy his parents an anniversary gift, and Mom a birthday gift. Shouldn't that've been Olivia's job to remember? At least to buy them a card. He couldn't do everything, especially when he'd been dead this week. Oh well, he'd be covering the bill tonight.

. . .

Mote:

Don't need reasons to give or receive presents. Life is a gift. Give freely.

CHAPTER
TWELVE

12. RAINE

Raine pulled up to their apartment building to find Lucid waiting just inside the vestibule door. She'd feared he'd be late, maybe stressing out over what shirt to wear or something, changing back and forth in a discussion with colors.

They were going to their grandparents' anniversary/grandma's birthday party. Lucid didn't drive, so when Raine got off work, she drove from North Hollywood back to Echo Park to pick him up. She'd closed Consumia's Spiritual Emporium last night and got home after Lucid had already gone to bed, then opened again this morning, pulling a "clo-pen."

When Lucid saw her, he galloped out and hurried into what he called their "commuter-egg," a safe place from loose city words that would be constantly launching themselves at them.

ROB WELDON

"Work's good," he said, anticipating her question. "The words and colors are friendlier."

"Is the job good on its own accord?" Raine said. "Or do you mean your relationship with Omnist II?"

He thought for a moment. "Both. I find working there to be an erotic activity." He said this as disaffectedly as saying he counted forty-nine customers through the middle hours of the day.

Raine was trying to work out what he meant.

"I can carry heavy things," Lucid continued. "Unbox and count anything I want. They let me arrange things on the shelves, especially when I have to make Obdurationals comfortable."

Obdurationals were stubborn words, but that didn't sound so erotic, unless he was talking about being turned on by numbers or organization. That wouldn't really surprise her. If he said the concept of the number three turned him on more than the number four, like he had some form of prime number fetish, she would accept that. "I'll admit I thought you meant something else," she said. "I thought you were talking about the Consumerians. The girls that come in there."

"I sweep and mop, too." As if she hadn't spoken. "Stock the bathroom. They said they're going to train me to use the register."

Raine was still stuck on this "erotic" comment. Lucid was neurodivergent, nearly anyone would notice, but as far as she knew, he had no sexual fetishes. He'd been seen by many doctors over the years, ever since he'd started school and his social phobias took center stage. It was almost a game with him, these visits. The doctors would ask him questions he said didn't match the flelling words around them, and he'd either remain silent or laugh at them.

"Like they think I can't tell," he'd say afterward. "But the nurses, they're nice. They're honest with me."

At one appointment in particular, when Lucid was eighteen and they'd just moved into the apartment together, Dr. Dore had pulled Raine aside and instructed her to watch out for further signs of oviphilia, a sexual fetish Raine would rather have not known existed. There was no casual way to introduce oviphilia into conversation with Lucid. For example, "Have you ever fantasized about a woman inserting a chicken egg into her vagina, then laying it for you? It could be a colored egg. Dyed. Anything you want." Then the person with the fetish, usually male, would eat the egg.

And if the answer was no, then she feared the act of asking the question would give him the idea. She could inadvertently create a monster. A man-child at twenty-one, Lucid was certainly a virgin. But he could be a virgin with curious fetishes and fantasies. Who knew what he did inside that egg-bed of his?

She would never ask.

Lucid described a woman he saw last night by the name of Sydnee. He'd seen her at the store the last two days. "She asked if I was going to morph into a butterfly," he said. "Imagine that. I like that. Instead of just the world changing colors around me, I could, too."

Raine didn't respond. The woman could've been making sexually suggestive comments, or she could be just as awkward at conversation as Lucid was.

"And Lucador kept being mean to me," Lucid said.

"Lucador's a unique character," Raine said. "He treats everyone the same, especially people he likes."

"He'd say things he wanted her to overhear." Lucid so rarely talked about a girl that Raine wanted to simultaneously warn him and allow him to feel encouraged. A flirty woman may boost his ego, even if she didn't want to date him. "I saw words like 'jealous' and 'insecure.'"

"All souls need company," Raine said. "Even loners often look for soulmates."

"Sydnee didn't come to talk to Lucador; she came for Vogel Grey. She was dressed so pretty."

"Sydnee or Vogel?"

"Huh." Lucid thought for a moment. "Sydnee. But I liked what Vogel was wearing, too."

They drove in silence for a moment as Raine negotiated from the 5 North onto the 134 West.

"My bandages kept falling off," Lucid said. "Sydnee helped wrap me back up. I told her I was sorry I was falling apart. The bandages were faulty. She said they're not faults, they're features. Features all over me. We laughed about this."

"She sounds nice."

"Then later Lucador said I was really called *Losed*, like a loser who 'loozed.' Not Lucid."

"That's horrible."

"And he laughed and laughed. 'HaHAA!'" His impersonation of Lucador was spot on.

"We laugh at what we fear," Raine said. "At our own qualities we see reflected in others, and what we find unfamiliar— both the scary-familiar, and the scary-strange. Lucador has a horrible sense of humor, but I bet he was joking. It was performative."

She didn't understand Lucid's attraction to Lucador. Lucid seemed to look up to him. Maybe he saw Lucador as a loner who'd found the strength to succeed on his own terms, by not following norms.

"He said real men don't wear tights," Lucid said. "And he'd just said I was a real man a couple days ago."

Lucid had shown Raine what he was going to wear last

night before she'd gone to work. He'd begun wearing black ballet tights when he was a small child, after taking a few ill-advised ballet lessons that ended in tears. But he continued wearing the tights, sometimes under his pants. They seemed to relax him the way his Soother-Wrap vests did. And last night, they *were* his pants. He'd also worn acrobatic shoes, the kind that were bendy and looked like high-tops that hugged his upper ankles. These were basically the equivalent of Soother-Wrap shoes with extra grippy soles. He said they allowed him to walk silently and leap from buildings like a superhero.

In a way, he'd worn a Soother-Wrap outfit. He should've been relatively comfortable.

"At first, I couldn't wait to hear what Vogel had to say," Lucid said. "Everything there was black and white. The store, the clothes."

"And she spoke about color, right?"

"Yes. She'd had us cover up most of the colors in the No-Basil Alcove with black or white sheets. It was like Omnist II had morphed into a living coloring book. It was a perfect place for her to invite them all back." He breathed a little harder. He was working himself up. "But she ruined it. It wasn't for the colors. She said they don't exist!"

First of all. Colors existed, didn't they? And second, if they didn't, you shouldn't say that to Lucid.

"And then Sydnee held my hand," he said.

Raine looked at him to gauge his emotions. Things like anger, frustration, confusion, or delight. There was nothing to see. He never touched anyone, much less held hands.

"She danced, right there next to me, twisting her hips so her dress kept hitting my leg, and I didn't mind."

Could Raine believe that it hadn't bothered him? Was he growing up?

"But even after we prayed to the goddess Vida Chroma and danced, everything was still black and white. The colors were angry that Vogel said they didn't exist. I had to save them! My head expanded to the size of the room, to protect the concept of color from those who wanted it dead. If Vogel believes colors only exist in my head, then my head needs to be big enough to absorb everything around me. Take in the whole world. If I put everything inside my head, the colors will all be safe. And Sydnee. She's nice. She was safe in my head, too."

"You realize that's opposite of an egg, right?" Raine said. "Instead of shutting yourself down inside a protective barrier, you expanded your walls until you became one with your environment."

"So that's bad?" Lucid so rarely made eye contact that his staring at her telegraphed importance.

"No, that's good."

"But I couldn't keep my head that big," Lucid said. "It took too much energy and too many malicious words were sneaking in, so I ran home."

"That probably confused everyone." Raine imagined pieces of white bandages flapping in the wind as he ran. "I'm sorry the Lodge ended so poorly for you."

Lucid believed in colors. Needed them. *Take them away at your own peril.*

THEY'D EXITED the freeway and were on Ventura Boulevard. Lucid's phone buzzed with a notification.

"I thought you were going to remove the Omnist after we talked about it," Raine said. The Omnist had that effect on people sometimes. Addictive qualities.

Lucid read the notification to himself. A few moments of silence.

Traffic was bad. They were late. She was almost never late for anything. She reached to turn on the radio, but Lucid waved his hand to stop her. "I like how it sometimes snows random words." He was referring to the Omnist. "'Learn to distinguish between personal beliefs and personal delusions,'" he recited. Paused. "You said that before."

Raine's favorite Motes inspired multiple interpretations, but this one sounded more like a fortune cookie with useful advice. "That's correct," she said. "I have indeed said that before. Like you, I'm far too young to be wise, but I endeavor to transform experience into wisdom."

Lucid seemed to be looking at the sky as if it were a movie screen. In awe. "I didn't even see those flelling," he said. "You're the best I've seen at nabbing words from the ether."

"Look inside you," Raine said. "Not all the words are out here in the environment. Some are inside. I keep mine on tiny hooks, thousands of them, on the inner walls of my soul. We always think of our soul as resting inside our body, but once you're there, you can then go deeper, as well. That's where I keep my words, inside my own levels of infinite regression."

This seemed to upset him. "You're calling me a yolk," he said.

"No, Lucid. I'm saying you're safe in there. All the nutrients you need for your mind and soul are inside you."

"I want to go home." He'd flipped on a dime. This happened sometimes; better than on an airplane, but worse now for their trip being complete.

"We're already here." Raine parked in the street about a block away from the restaurant. "We have to go in."

"I've used up all the words." But he obviously had enough

left to say that. Like electronics that had enough power left to run low-battery lights.

Raine turned off the car. "Everyone wants to see you. And you have lots to talk about... your new job, last night's Lodge... Sydnee." She took a wrapped gift from the backseat.

"I just want my egg," Lucid said.

THIRTEEN

13. LUCADOR

Tim and Eileen were Executive Saint believers of the darkest magic associated with either the Emporium or Omnist II, but they balanced that out by also being two of the more gregarious Consumerians Lucador knew. They were purchasing a translucent but partially smoked crystal shaped like the head of Lucador's PGA-illegal two-way chipper golf head. The story card taped to the crystal promised the smoky image was a demon was trapped inside. Eileen set it on the counter.

"The demon, it makes you happy?" Lucador said, standing next to them like he was part of their transaction.

"You know," Eileen said, "it actually does."

Kick typed a PO number from the story card into the computer.

"You should buy the *empty* crystals to put the demons in,"

Lucador said. "Not the already filled-up ones! This is like buying used paint!"

Kick shot Lucador a look.

"But look at it!" Tim said, lifting the crystal and turning it. "The demon's so ugly! It's amazing."

"Don't worry, honey," Eileen said to Tim. "You're still uglier!"

"Hey!" Tim said. "I resemble that remark!"

Kick adjusted his thick-framed glasses and scratched his beard as he glared at Lucador. It was a common thinking action he did when he was biting his tongue. This bothered Lucador. He preferred looks of approval when he was on stage and looks of attentiveness when he was speaking over looks of judgment when he was standing out in the open like this. He was an exposed target.

"Like this morning!" Lucador said. "I saw the demon in my toast! Just as trapped! The bread and heat had tripped the snare! No crystal vessel needed!"

"Your breakfast caused an exorcism in me," Tim said to Eileen. "In the porcelain vessel!"

Eileen took the crystal from Tim and pretended to stab him with it while Kick turned the register tablet around for her to sign.

"I'm surprised you didn't bring the toast in to try to sell it," Kick said to Lucador.

"Sell it?" Lucador rubbed his stomach. "It was breakfast!"

"Speaking of which, we're on our way to dinner," Eileen said, as they headed for the door. She waved at Kick and Lucador with the crystal, no bag needed. "What do you think the demon wants to eat?"

Tim shrugged. "Soul food?"

"Have an Omniscient day!" Kick said with worry on his face. He never made jokes like this. He placed one hand on the counter and groaned as he rubbed the back of his wrist against his eyebrows. Odd way to itch the forehead.

"Why do you make the moaning?" Lucador said. *Kick needs to let it out; he holds too much in.* "The more I talk, the more you make noises of the tired."

"Don't tell customers not to buy our merchandise, please," Kick said.

"The crystal? They still bought it. I'm just making the conversation." This was good customer service. Kick should know this.

"Then why don't you take over the register for a while? You can talk till your little heart's content." Kick said. "And that bag. Why don't you take that off and stay a while?"

"This?" Lucador patted the leather bag worn messenger-style across his chest. It was the new one he'd been working on in his garage. "Keeping it warm."

It was no secret Lucador talked a lot. Standard mode. Factory settings. Kick had told him once that Lucador needed a filter between his stream of consciousness and the words that came out, but Kick was unaware how much the pressure built up and caused pain. How restrained words itched uncomfortably in the brain. Sometimes squirmy words found their way out no matter which filter he applied. An example: "Did you see her holding hands with the boy?"

"Yeah, so that means Sydnee wasn't here for you last night," Kick said, resuming his work on his laptop. "She really was looking for Lucid."

"Impossible she looks for him. She's a Lucadorian. She's been here before, always for me." Even when Lucador wasn't swinging a sword, he wished he were. It helped him project his voice, adding gravity to the words, and people took him more seriously. "You see the way she stares." Kick wasn't looking. It was driving him crazy. "And he's just a boy."

"He's twenty-one."

"He's egg salad."

That made Kick look. Everyone had a button. Find it and press to get a reaction. "Be nice," he said. "We're here to protect and encourage him."

"No one protects him more than me!" Lucador said. "I am the mentor; the best one he's ever had! We're practically the same!"

"You can't be serious. You guys are opposites. Your names are similar, that's it."

"Lucid, he says it was the words, the words *themselves*, that chose us to cross the paths. And I believe him! The boy doesn't lie; he cannot lie! I understand him better than the teachers, better than the parents. Maybe more than Raine! His mother, she's too permissive. Soft rules make the soft child! Sheep! No participation trophies at Omnist II! Lucadorians keep score, otherwise how do you know who wins? And what kind of a name is 'Lucid'?"

"Wow," Kick said. "So much to unpack there. Where do we begin? First of all, he was born Lewis, after his grandfather."

Lucador would've known this if he'd been the one to fill out the employment forms with Lucid, but that was for the egghead lovers of the bureaucratic, like Kick.

"Was he the punisher? Who toughens the boy?" Lucador said. "Lucid said he sees the words, and I say the words make the man! If he was my son, I'd name him Fuller. That way he sees the blood groove every time he sees his name, Fuller Oxford!"

"But if he was your son, he'd be Fuller San Lucador."

"You know what I mean. I'll show you." Lucador waved him off and retrieved a sword from a display and set it on the counter. "Look at this." He ran his finger down the middle groove that ran the length of it. "This is the blood groove; they call it a fuller, to help the blood flow after you stab. No more suction, too, so you can pull it out and stab again." He pretended to elbow an assailant behind him. "Or defend! HaHAA!"

"Good to know." But Kick didn't look all that impressed.

"So we have the goal!" Lucador said. "We'll teach the boy to defend!"

"You're really getting into this. Are you having paternal urges or something?"

"I do not urge, and I'll never marry. Waste of time! My knowledge is for everyone. I'm everyone's surrogate dad! And look what I build for Lucid. Come, come, I'll show you. He'll like this."

Lucador escorted Kick to the Forgery and showed him what looked like a cross between a couple sets of heavy-duty industrial shelves and a woodshop treehouse. He'd made or salvaged items from his garage, transporting the monstrosity over in three pieces to fashion together in the corner of the Forgery. He'd waited for Lucid to leave before bringing the pieces in the back door. It had only taken a few minutes.

"Omnist Egg," Lucador said proudly. It wasn't majestic; he knew this. But it would be awe-inspiring for the boy.

"Looks like a mansion for a cat," Kick said.

"He *is* the cat. He can hide and scratch. And watch." Lucador got on his hands and knees and crawled into the elongated complex. His belly barely fit inside. "Can you see my eyes?"

"No."

"HaHAA! It works! I can see the whites of your eyes. If I had a rifle, you'd be dead!"

"And if I had a dirty chai tea, I'd be awake."

Lucador was stuck in the Omnist Egg. Not that he was wedged in tight, but he couldn't turn around. He'd built this for someone much skinnier. It was an art piece, but also a sort of casket you entered at the foot. That's what the boy would want. Backing his way out took Lucador a lot longer than crawling in.

THE WOMAN OF THE HOUR, Sydnee, walked through the front door and Lucador practically leapt over a couch in the No-Basil Alcove to greet her.

"My," she said, slowing at his encroachment.

"Yours," he said, taking off his new leather satchel, the strap catching over his head and pulling a chunk of his black, pomade-greasy hair down over his cheekbone. The bag was branded with Lucador's logo, as in, literally branded with an iron. They sold similar bags in the store. Big ticket items.

"My," she said again, apparently at a loss for words. She held the bag away from her body as Lucador patted it like a pet. "Thank you, Empty."

"Empty? I'm not the Empty!"

"I thought you were Emptor San Lucador the First?" Sydnee said. "It's a nickname."

"No emptiness; I am filled with everything! But your satchel; *it* is empty! You can use it for your exorcism things; now it's a kit! You can add to it! I make the blades for your spells: athames and bolines down that aisle!" Kick would be impressed with how he was using a gift to make the upsell. Like free fruit tea selling more kombucha.

"What a surprise," she said. "I barely know you."

"I see you at my Lodges! A Lucadorian to the core! But last night—" he waved a dismissive hand— "I was the color commentator." He paused as he processed his comment. "HaHAA! Sí! I added the color to Vogel's black and white!"

"Thank you again, Mr. First," Sydnee said, lowering the satchel. "Well, I was hoping that young man Lucid was working today? The handsome man in tights?"

No! I bear the gift, yet she looks elsewhere! I should take it back! Last night, Lucador had been dressed properly and manly. A black leather vest, a puffy white button-up shirt, a cape. Grey wool pants. Layers. But he never wore tights or leggings like the child-man-boy. And of course, Sydnee had focused on the tights. *The heathens!*

"The Lucid boy, he's not here," Lucador said. "I think he's scared of the crowd out there!" He gestured out the window to some kids out front on the sidewalk, vaping, drinking kombucha, waiting for this evening's Lodge with Imani Chartreuse. One was wearing a funny hat that looked like a broken shell with the top removed, revealing whites and yolks for brains. Like he was on his way to a college football game. *The Ducks! The Chickens! The Eggheads!* Whatever those team names were. Lucid would never gather with those kids; he was too shy, too skittish. But Sydnee was sure to be impressed with Omnist II's fanbase, clearly spillover from Lucador's successful Lodges.

"He's at his grandparents' party," Kick said.

"Sí!" Lucador said. "Eating the appetizers of birthday anniversaries!"

"I see," Sydnee said. "I'll come back tomorrow, then. Thank you again for the bag."

"No, no," Lucador said. "The Lodge is in an hour! The Cosmic Egg Omniscian, Imani Chartreuse. Lucid would like her, so maybe you like her, too."

FOURTEEN

14. RAINE

The rest of the family was gathered at the bar awaiting the kids' arrival. The grandparents, Lewis and Marian, both looked comfortable in their element. Grandpa was smiling and happy, Grandma scowling and happy. Dad held a posture that communicated he was running this event, and Olivia was sitting with her hands together, quiet and polite, like she had been groomed to be seen, not heard.

Being the more social of the siblings, Raine stepped up to greet the grandparents, Grandma garnering extra time for birthday wishes. The gift Raine was holding was large, but small enough to have been kept tucked under an arm for the requisite hugs. She then stepped aside so they could attack Lucid with cheers and squeezes. They still treated him like he was a child. He'd usually shrink away from these sorts of advances, but she could tell he was trying to be a good sport.

Raine now handed over Grandma's present. It was covered in many pieces of red and gold Japanese rice paper, each the size of a small paperback novel, so she'd had to tape them on one by one.

"Oh, sweetie, thank you," Grandma said, setting it on the bar. "I'll save it for after dinner."

"Noooo!" Grandpa said. "Open it now! What's the fun in waiting?" He picked it up and shook it. There was no sound. "Is it a puppy?"

"Oh, Lewis!" Grandma said.

"If it is, we better let it out!" He looked over at Olivia, the newest audience addition for his sitting-down stand-up, who was doing her best Mona Lisa impersonation.

"Okay, fine." Grandma took the gift. She began trying to arduously remove each sheet of paper individually, as if trying not to tear them, and it was taking forever.

"Come on, Marian, hurry it up!" Grandpa said.

"I'll get there when I get there," she said. "Raine put a lot of effort into wrapping this."

"For you to rip off!" He was overjoyed at the prospect, and reached over and tore the top sheets clean off. Lucid and Raine laughed. Olivia was smiling. Dad was zoning out.

Grandma pulled down the rest of the paper and was clearly confused by what she was holding. It was wooden, painted black, gold, and red, and shaped like a squished pi symbol a few inches tall and about eighteen inches long.

"It's an Egyptian headrest, like the one I use," Raine said.

Grandma turned it over in her hands. "It's beautiful."

"Linden at CSE built it, but Lucid and I decorated it. We added lots of small details."

"It's really wonderful, darling," Grandma said, leaning over to kiss both grandchildren, but Lucid lay back and nodded. "It'll have to go on the mantel in the living room. I don't know if at my age in life I should be messing with my neck when I sleep."

"That's what this is for. It helps correct your spine. It helps with a stiff back and neck."

"I mean, I'm not changing my sleep pattern at seventy-five. I like my pillows."

THEY COULD'VE BEEN at a table already if they'd wanted, but apparently, Dad didn't want the party seated until the kids arrived. So they were still at the bar. Grandma Marian was about to have a coronary over it. Really, though, Raine suspected Dad wanted to watch a television out of the corner of his eye.

Finally, Dad lifted his drink, as if toasting. "My parents and my children."

Olivia smiled, apparently oblivious to being left out of the toast.

"Time to be seated," he said, rather anti-climatically.

"Ayyyyy!" Grandpa said, which sounded like he was cele-brating Dad's comment, but he was looking toward the door.

Raine's mom, Geta, had just walked in with a date, a man Raine didn't immediately recognize, but whose identity she could guess based on what she'd heard. Mom was dressed well in wrinkle-free slacks and an overly shiny shirt, an outfit which may have been purchased with this particular event in mind. Mom went up to her ex-parents-in-law first, kissing each of them on the cheek while bestowing congratulations. They enthusiastically received her.

"It's been way too long!" Grandma Marian said.

"I don't care what anyone says," Grandpa Lewis said. "You'll always be our daughter!"

Raine looked over at Dad to gauge his response, but he was looking at a television. Listening, probably, but pretending he wasn't.

Mom held her arms wide to telegraph to Lucid she was coming in for a hug. He was never someone who liked surprise touches, not even a tap on the shoulder. He submitted to the embrace, maybe even smiling at Mom's surprise appearance. Mom made "yummy" noises while squeezing him.

Raine and her mom didn't have an icy relationship by any means. They were just different people. Their hug was barely more than chins over each other's shoulders, but accompanied by authentic smiles.

"You smell like a smoothie," Mom whispered, as if it were a secret to which no one else was privy. It was true, though. Raine preferred natural scents; not artificial chemicals intended to smell authentic, but the actual essences or oils of things found in nature. She pulled scents out of the ether the way Lucid did with words. Her selections were often food-inspired. Today's mixture included blackberry and vanilla.

"Heaven is what we smell," Raine said. Mom was wearing a nearly overpowering high-end fragrance. How she could smell the subtleness of what Raine was wearing, she could only guess. Mom smelled like a lie. "That's why it's our most acute sense."

"You're so precious," Mom said, then turned away. "William." She nodded but didn't kiss or hug him, then gestured to her date. "Everybody, this is Ryan."

He was clean-cut, his white hair clustered with dark grey near the ears. He wore business attire in a nonchalant way that communicated this was casual for him. The couple was well-matched. Raine had heard Mom talk about Ryan, but she'd never met him.

Everyone greeted him, with Dad coming across most corporate. Except Lucid was staring at the new man. Reading words, maybe. Analyzing colors.

"Didn't know if you were going to make it," Grandpa said with an upturned inflection, like it was half question and half statement. Raine hadn't heard anybody in the party inquire about Mom's whereabouts, though. Mom hadn't been expected.

"Well, Ryan here convinced me not to miss a party with my children and their grandparents. It's all so appropriate." Mom was halfway to becoming Grandma Marian, even though they weren't related. Mom was a good person, but raising someone she considered a high-maintenance child had hardened her, made her sterner and more demanding. She was now blossoming around other adults, rather than sequestering herself with school-aged children.

"What, exactly, is 'appropriate'?" Dad said.

"These people—just *look* at you!" Mom said, ignoring Dad and holding her arms out like she was going to hug the anniversary couple again. Grandpa Lewis pretended to look behind him to see who she was talking to. Grandma Marian was smirking, loving the attention. "Some of us are aging so well," Mom said, patting Grandma Marian's shoulder.

"Well, I'm glad you made it," Dad said, apparently changing tack. A perfect, flat-toned statement honed in business meetings concerning quarterly numbers.

"My, aren't you easy on the eyes," Mom said, still ignoring Dad as she turned back to Raine. Even though her statement was about her daughter, it was really about herself. Mom was the one drawing and directing everyone's attention. "I love this dress. One of yours?"

Raine often tweaked vintage clothing to suit her own taste. Usually dresses. This was a free-flowing sundress of multiple shades of blues, purple, and white. "I'm here to please and be pleased," she said, mocking a curtsy.

"You're not at work, honey," Mom said, changing tone. "Relax, have a drink."

She loved her mom, but often found her pushy at family events. The desire to be a hostess, mannered and proper, directing behavior. She much preferred Mom one on one, when it was less of a performance.

"But you look great, too," Raine said to deaf ears. "Did you—"

"And Lucid, do you need anything?" Mom held on to his forearm, as if he would wander away without being tethered. "Do you have your headphones with you?"

Of course. She was already setting her son aside. Lucid's basic resting face was a look of consternation, but now a subtle wince poked through. Given permission to be antisocial, he stuck earbuds in his ears and started playing with his phone. It wasn't even like Mom did this so she could talk about him without him hearing. She just wanted him preoccupied.

"He should be free to fly with the words or he'll always resent you," Raine said. "The way a patient begins to resent his crutches."

"Sweetheart," Mom said. "Don't be jealous."

As if Raine had a jealous bone in her body. As if jealousy were a physical part of the human anatomy. As if this had anything, at all, to do with jealousy. She often caught Mom not really paying attention to what she'd just said, like now. Really, this happened to her with nearly everyone when Raine elevated the conversation beyond small talk. Some people were uninterested in level-jumping, especially in mixed company, or when they took her suggestion as an insult to their intelligence.

As an example, her boss Connie level-jumped when talking about the Emporium. Kick, when talking about virality of ideas, technology, and games. With Lucid, Raine could level-jump about many things. Not everything—not girls or mainstream pop culture he wasn't familiar with—but nearly everything else. They often talked about concepts far more important, like life, death, family, language, music, fine art, and symbols.

Mom's modus operandi was to placate Lucid. If he showed her a vibrantly colored painting he'd made, a representation of his current worldview, Mom would say, "That's nice, honey," and mean it, but she'd add nothing to the conversation.

By contrast, Raine would ask what moods the colors represented today. What words they were catching or avoiding. Et cetera. His artwork was a conversation starter, not a completed statement. In this way, words healed Lucid.

That's what this is; Mom is placatory. "That's nice, sweetie," *comes out of her mouth as easily as* "Don't be jealous."

The bartender brought Mom a cabernet and Ryan a Tom Collins.

"Isn't it life-affirming to see Lewis and Marian together for fifty years?" Mom said, as she held up her beverage in a mock toast, not unlike the one Dad had just made. She wasn't toasting, exactly, but wanted the attention a toast would generate.

"It is," Raine said. "Life itself is life-affirming." She'd written that as a Mote. "It sounds redundant, but it isn't. And it would be a self-fulfilling prophecy, if only it were a prophecy."

"My dear Raine," Mom said. "Aren't you wonderful?" She raised her voice to make sure everyone was listening. "Isn't she wonderful? My daughter, the healer."

"Hear, hear!" Grandpa said.

"A fine young lady," Grandma said.

"I'm here to happy and be happy." A twist on what she'd said earlier, but there was no noticeable response from Mom this time.

CHAPTER
FIFTEEN

15. LUCADOR

Part-time Omnist II employee Elijah walked up to Kick and Lucador, holding a stack of story cards stamped with red Omnist II logos. "I think I got them all," he said. He was wearing a button-up checked shirt with pearl snaps, tucked into brown pants with a belt. The pants seemed a little crooked, like he needed to rotate them a half an inch clockwise. He seemed a bit naïve to Lucador, but fearless when it came to talking to women or asking spiritual questions. Distractable, but a good employee.

"Those go on the merchandise!" Lucador said. A red logo designated inexpensive items, things twenty-five dollars and under. Red meant "Stop, don't buy! Keep on shopping!" A green logo was for merchandise over a hundred dollars. Green meant "Go ahead and buy!" Prices in between were black. The color coding was Lucador's idea, and a fine one, if he had to say so himself. Kept the shoppers in the upper echelon of price, where they belonged.

"Yeah, we know," Elijah said. "Your protégé stamped red logos for green prices."

"Impossible!" Lucador said. "He is the color expert! And a number wizard!"

Elijah handed him one of the cards. Red stamp, but it had a price of $250 on it. Probably for a Lucadorian sword or leather bag. Couldn't argue with that; they'd have to make new cards.

"We think he was seeing red as green yesterday," Kick said.

"I'll talk to the boy," Lucador said. "No need for you to get between us!"

"Will you text him now?!" Kick said. "I don't mind doing it."

"Put them back on the merchandise! We're too busy for people to think everything is free!" Lucador said, waving them off, suddenly hungry and grumpy. "We'll fix them tomorrow!"

TONIGHT'S OMNISCIAN was Imani Chartreuse. She was small with dark skin, dark hair, dark eyes, and wore a white shirt and brown skirt. Her clothes almost made her look like one of the organic eggs they sold at Omnist II.

Imani's in-store merchandise included crystal eggs, painted wooden egg-rests, hand-woven baskets, strainers, a recipe book with an "origin of the universe" introduction, posters of giant levitating eggs in landscapes and cityscapes, life-sized egg keychains (realistic or multicolored), egg-framed sunglasses, and novelty hats. Like most Omniscians, she peddled an assortment of T-shirts, but hers were humorous, one-paneled memes printed on cotton. An example was a galaxy that looked like a fried egg. Overall, her items were more playful than the average Omniscian's.

"Welcome from the ocean," Imani said, standing on the stage's drum riser. She'd joked with Lucador that she wanted to stand there because she was vertically challenged and had expressed a desire to see the crowd in its entirety. "Welcome from the womb. Welcome from the conception of life. From all the galactic, primordial, and bacterial soups. All the places from which we come."

Lucador was hungry. It smelled like dinner was cooking in Omnist II. Vegetable broth with potatoes, celery, onions, and carrots. *Hurry, chef!*

"The Cosmic Egg speaker," Lucador said to Kick, standing on the customer side of the front counter, facing the stage. "The boy should be here for this. She speaks his language."

"You know there's more to Imani than just saying the word 'egg,' right?" Kick said.

"Of course!" *She's a chef, too!*

Imani spoke about how various cultures, pre-science, explained reproduction, from babies carried by storks to men themselves carrying the egg and planting it like a seed into a woman.

"These aren't new ideas. They're ancient. Virtually all cultures have myths and traditions that involve eggs and reproduction—even before we knew that women literally carry eggs inside them—and the origins and continuation of life.

"The earliest forms of life began as single cells, and that's what a cell is, a microscopic egg. Which came first, you ask, the chicken or the egg? That's easy. The egg. Eggs existed long before a creature that we call a chicken."

Satisfied she had everyone's attention, Imani stepped down from the riser and to the side of the stage where there was a three-gallon cauldron heating on a large electric hotplate. This was the source of the appetizing dinner aroma. She stirred the contents with a ladle and continued her speech.

"The universe began as a cosmic egg, a blast that hatched all matter, all the galaxies of suns and planets. You know how some fish spray their eggs into the water like little bursts of living supernovae? It's like that." She stirred again and looked at the audience intensely, as if asked a question. "Am I losing you?"

Lucador looked around to see if he was the only one getting lost, getting hungry. He saw Sydnee standing by herself, her satchel strapped properly, messenger bag-style across her chest. She'd put on a floppy hat like an olive-skinned southern belle.

Great news! She comes back! Maybe she'd like some soup!

Lucador was trying to get Sydnee's attention by performing his *posta* drill with a sword in her line of sight. Although it wasn't a fire capacity event, maybe half full, there were still too many people for him to perform a cycle of guards safely. He realized Imani had stopped talking and was looking at him. "No, no, please continue," he said. "A practice of guards is silent!"

Imani sighed. Lucador sheathed his sword and attempted to follow along.

"The earth is one of these drifting fish eggs in the galactic soup," Imani said, "and within the earth's own gumbo of elements, single cells swirled like clouds of little eggs, and life emerged from these eggs, more complex, more complex, until finally here we are. And we women, as infants, contain all the eggs we'll need in our lifetimes. But all of us, everything we see, began as an egg."

Imani opened a carton of Omnist II organic eggs. There

were six stacks of egg-shaped mugs on a folding table next to the cauldron.

"Eggs can be dangerous, too, like a hot, exploding egg. Have you heard about this? Let's say you made some hard-boiled eggs yesterday and kept them in the fridge. You take one out today and put it in a bowl of water to reheat in the microwave. Water will keep the egg from exploding in the microwave. The bell dings and you take it out and set it down carefully on your plate, and then BAM! Once it's disturbed or poked, it explodes with a huge popping noise. Burning pieces of egg magma fly everywhere and your face gets covered in molten breakfast. Maybe some of it gets in your eye and blinds you." She raised her ladle, not unlike Lucador would do. "Beware of the attacking egg!"

Lucador liked this. They should join forces and create a part-ladle-part-knife Lucadorian utensil for her to push at her events elsewhere. A ladle with a hilt? A retractable blade? He'd have to work this out later.

"Luc, you are Omnist II's exploding egg," Kick said, a verbal nudge to his ribcage.

"HaHAA! You burned me!" His signature rebel yell caused a few people to turn. Even his whispers were punctuated by exclamation marks. Sydnee didn't look this time, though.

"Look at this," Imani said, holding an egg lengthwise between her thumb and forefinger for the crowd to see. "This galactic soup will become an egg drop gumbo." She cracked the egg on the side of the cauldron and added it to the soup. "Helps to stir it first, get the broth flowing, like time in a circle. Around and around." She added another egg. "Spiritual broth. See that carrot?"

No, nobody could see inside the cauldron on the stage.

"Ingredients rise to the surface, appearing for a glance at our world, then sink back below. But not forgotten. The ingredients are still there, swimming in context. Nourishing vita-mins. A cauldron of life, and life is food. Life feeds on life. But life does so in order to beget more life. Is there more life on the planet than before? Do we net more life in this existential equation?"

She chopped this idea of life to a simple egg and rebuilt from there. Then the fittest survive! The fighters! Genius!

She put the last egg into the cauldron of soup. The eggshells had filled one of her egg-mugs on the table. "Our heads are like the microwave-heated eggs, and we keep packing them with information until what's inside grows too big, exploding with new bombshell discoveries. We contain language until it bursts into new dialects. We contain our patience, simmering our emotions until we explode out of our social shells of politeness. We are kept contained in our youth, in a family unit, in school, or within our peer group—until what? We break free of those, too. We burst forth into adult-hood. The egg is a universal symbol of life, nature, and knowledge."

Imani took a new egg-mug and ladled some soup into it. "We often say we're fried when we're tired. We're scrambled when we're confused. We're raw when we're inexperienced. So, maybe we will end up as another form of egg when we die. Like us, eggs have evolved, and now contain more nutrients, more calories. But the shape and structure remain remarkably the same."

Imani nodded at Elijah, who stepped onto the stage, took the ladle from her, and began filling mugs.

"Line up and share some egg drop soup with me," Imani said. "All you have to do is buy a mug and you get the soup for free. There's no other animal product in it, besides the egg, if you have dietary restrictions." Imani handed her first mug to an audience member in the front row.

Kick was right; Lucador should text Lucid. But not about the mis-stamped story cards. The boy was missing out even more than he thought; Imani was perfect for him. But first, Lucador would enjoy a mug of soup. He cut his way to the front of the line. No waiting for him. He was co-owner, after all. *And maybe next time, Imani will make breakfast burritos!*

CHAPTER
SIXTEEN

16. RAINE

After they'd been seated, Ryan engaged Lucid in conversation, which meant the earbud on Ryan's side of Lucid's head had been taken out, but the other was still in. Ryan appeared to be trying. Not annoyingly hard, but a as good guy wanting to get along with his girlfriend's son. They were talking about jazz, an appropriate topic. Mom was engaged with the grandparents as if there'd never been a divorce. Lots of touching of hands, arms, and shoulders.

"You'd think hitting the fly three times with a newspaper would kill it!" Grandpa said.

"You would think!" Mom said. "But I've got some *news* for you!"

Grandpa's laugh was so velvety that, even though it was often louder than the others, it sounded easier. Well broken in. Years of practice. Raine wondered if all of his life were edited down to only the time spent laughing, how long of a duration would that be? It would add up to multiple years. And when Grandpa wasn't sure whether it was time to laugh yet, he would listen with his head tilted back and open his mouth, anticipating his cue.

"And it still wasn't dead!" Grandma said. "It just continued on like nothing happened!"

Grandpa laughed again. It softened the potential ice between Mom and Dad, Mom and Olivia. Dad didn't look well. He'd withdrawn from the conversation.

Olivia was quiet as usual, bouncing her attention between the talkers and Dad as he stared into his glass of scotch. Was there trouble between them? Raine wanted to ask Lucid what words he saw flelling about them, but he was tied up with Ryan.

"Are you okay, Dad?" Raine said. "Silence is a virtue, but it's unlike you to be this way at a party."

He lifted his eyebrows at her. He'd been zoning out. She saw the same behavior at times with Lucid. Like she could've waved a hand in front of his face and he wouldn't have flinched.

"I'm fine, I'm fine," Dad said.

"He's been under the weather," Olivia said, lightly touching his arm. Her eyes were round and kind. She was a good soul.

Raine felt herself nodding. Sometimes people needed a break. Sometimes their souls needed sleep more than their bodies did.

"I was just thinking," Dad said. "Remember Santa Barbara? How I got there?"

She did.

THE EPISODE HAD BEGUN one morning when Mom stopped Dad while he was walking through the house naked. "William!" she said. "What are you doing? Go get dressed."

"Why?" he said. "No one can see me."

"I can see you just fine," Mom said. "And I don't like what I see. Go back to bed. I'll bring you some coffee."

"Dead people don't drink coffee. We don't eat. And we don't wear clothes."

"Just go back to bed. I'll be up there in a minute."

"We don't sleep, either."

Raine had been reading ghost stories in the living room and got up to see the spectacle of her father, the ghost. People had always said she floated when she walked, but she hadn't really known what they meant until that moment. He was a ghost rising up the stairs. Unassuming, unaware of his visibility, unashamed.

"Go sit down, sweetie," Mom said to Raine.

Raine learned years later that Dad had done this several times, and Mom's theory was that part of Dad's brain had awakened while the rest was still sleeping, and caffeine would wake him all the way up. In a way, that meant he was acting on a daydream, on a delusion. Then after the episode passed, he could get dressed and join the rest of the family like normal.

But when Mom had gone to the bedroom that morning with the coffee, he was gone. He'd grabbed his keys, snuck out the door, and driven away. They didn't hear from him until the next morning when Mom got a call that he was found sleeping naked on the beach near Santa Barbara. An early morning surfer had called the cops.

Dad didn't remember making the two-hour drive up there until after he'd spent a few hours sitting in the drunk tank, suddenly recalling everything, like the curtain had opened for him. He said it felt like someone else had done those things, not him. Like he had watched the events in a movie. Despite previously claiming he was dead, he'd now said he was lucky to be alive, the police having saved his life. Mom had to drive to Santa Barbara with his wallet and clothes before they would release him. His car had been parked illegally and towed, as well.

When he got home, he claimed to have had several revelations during the drive back. He was certain his destiny called for him to be more successful, to make more money, so that his family would love him more than ever. It was all about focus and determination on his end. If death could happen at any moment, he reasoned he was obligated to create his own heaven on earth before it was all taken away from him. Life was a delicate sand castle, and the next wave could come crashing in at any time. He said he was fortunate to live with a family so fortunate.

"Yes, the universe took care of you that day," Raine presently said.

"I'd thought I was a ghost," Dad said. "And I wasn't invisible; I know that. Obviously. Even if I'd actually died, you guys would've seen my body."

"William, living people can't be ghosts," Mom said.

Dad looked at Mom. She was needling him. In the past, this would've led to an argument. Olivia was listening intently. She may not have known the story.

"I assume you're going to elaborate on a larger point," Raine said.

"I'm just saying, that was the incident that led to our greatest conversation ever," Dad said. "I'd never felt closer to my family. Tonight may be all well and good, but it'll never be as great as that night."

Maybe this was Dad flexing in his bitterness at Mom for showing up and taking over as the engine of the party he'd put together for his parents. And if he'd been under the weather, like Olivia had said, he wouldn't be able to keep up with her.

Raine remembered the conversation the night after his Santa Barbara episode as feeling purgatorial, like the family had been sucked into a vortex created by a man who wasn't aware he was shifting the gravity around them, trapping everybody in a state of constant, painful emotional cleansing. He'd monologued, as if he were a preacher and the family a congregation hanging on his every word. Lucid, rapt and attentive, had devoured all of it, like he was being presented with gifts magically pulled from thin air. Raine, though, felt confined by a desperate man professing his love for them and the universe. The part where he professed his love wasn't the problem, but how and why he was doing it was. It had been painful.

"Words to remember," Raine said, looking for a response from the one-ear-budded Lucid. He seemed less relaxed, eyes roving the scene.

"I did it, though," Dad said, ignoring the question. "I did what I set out to do. I succeeded at business and provided well for my family. And what do I have to show for it? All I am to the family is a check...anymore, anyway."

Olivia turned her gaze down. Dad and she were twins now, both staring into their drinks. Raine didn't take the bait. Nor did Mom. But the flags were there; this night may not end well.

"William, that's enough," Grandma said.

"You did do a great job, William," Grandpa said. "You gave us wonderful grandkids."

Sitting between Grandpa and Olivia, Dad attempted

conviviality by standing up to make a toast again. "My people." He gazed around the table to make eye contact with each of the guests. "My past, present, and future are all here."

Unsure of where he was going with this, Raine expected him to say Olivia was pregnant.

Still holding up his glass, Dad reached down and plucked a half egg off Olivia's Caesar salad and popped it in his mouth. He may have forgotten he was mid-toast. "I love pickled eggs," he said.

"William," Grandma said, "that was hard boiled, not pickled."

He slammed the rest of his scotch. "Better?" he said, jiggling his torso, shaking the mixture inside him around. "It's pickled now!" Standing at his chair, with everyone else seated, this came off like a stage routine. He laughed. Ryan and Grandpa smiled. Grandma, Mom, and Olivia looked uncomfortable. Lucid looked like he always did: distracted, but probably listening.

"You make me see the world differently," Dad said to Raine, sucking his teeth and adopting a reverent tone. "Both of you," he corrected, gesturing at Lucid. "He swims in words and colors. You, Raine, in philosophy and spirituality. I...wonder...if..."

"If you can swim?" Grandpa said. Ryan laughed the hardest of the bunch. Mom's shoulders moved as if she'd punched Ryan in the knee to make him stop, even as an uncomfortable smile was hardwired to her face.

"...biologically..."

Raine was afraid Dad was going to have another episode. Tonight. He'd harbored some different ideas about biology that weren't rooted in science or popular belief, and his episodes had seemed to fortify that line of thinking.

ONE TIME when he was about eight years old, Lucid had fallen off his bike, faceplanting into the dead, dried skeleton of a neighbor's bush at the edge of the sidewalk. A hard, exposed root had stabbed his face and almost poked out his eye, missing it by a fraction of an inch. The doctor who stitched him up told him how lucky he was. The wood could've blinded him.

While Dad drove them home from the hospital, Lucid had a panic attack. Too many people in the emergency room had put him on edge, and the doctor was only trying to cheer him up when he told him how lucky he'd been. But Lucid kept dwelling on the accident, as if his eye had indeed been stabbed and he could no longer see from it.

"You needn't worry, Lucid," Dad had said. "If you have a glass eye in long enough, nerves will connect to it, anyway. You'll be able to see again."

SO MAYBE RAINE and Lucid had become Dad's glass eyes, his surrogate method of seeing the world. This uncomfortable toast was his way of pronouncing his love for them, publicly. She just wished he'd been sober when he said it.

Olivia tugged William's pants leg to get him to sit. He did, roughly.

"So, William," Mom said. "Remember how you said if you had a glass eye in your head long enough, nerves would connect to it?" She was thinking along the same line as Raine. Maybe Mom was trying to embarrass Dad in front of Ryan and Olivia, who were both listening attentively.

"Oh, I don't know," Dad said. "I said a lot of things."

"You said that the day Lucid got stitches right by his eye.

Remember that? Let's pretend you have a glass eye and optic nerves actually did connect to it. What do you think you'd see?"

He laughed nervously. "I'm no doctor."

"Just as a thought experiment," Mom said. "What would you see?"

"I imagine it would be like a fisheye lens. Maybe a portion of it would be in focus, and the rest would be like a bubble. A blurry bubble. I don't know. I was just playing around. Trying to cheer up Lucid."

This seemed to trigger Lucid, and Raine held his hand to keep him from running. He didn't have a bad relationship with Dad; there was never violence, emotional or physical, but it was a poor one, nonetheless. More neglectful than anything. Dad didn't seem built for closeness with his children, or anyone, really. She doubted Dad and Olivia were close. Theirs was likely a marriage of convenience.

"I don't need cheering up! No more scar, look!" Lucid pointed at the faint scar next to his eye. He jutted his face at Dad aggressively. She imagined Lucid deftly deflecting words with his chin and teeth.

"Scars aren't faults, honey," Mom said. "They're features. You're features all the way down, from head to toe."

That was it for Lucid. He pulled his hand away and got up from the table. Raine got up and followed him.

"Oh, come on, Lucid," Grandma said.

"Raine," Mom said.

Raine was making sure Lucid wasn't fleeing the restaurant, and when she saw him go into the restroom, she came back to the table to say her goodbyes.

"I don't know what I did," Mom said.

"The universe acts on its own," Raine said. "All we can do is respond."

"I don't even know what universe my son is *in*," Dad said. "I wasn't criticizing him."

"Nor was I," Mom said. She had an apologetic look on her face. She probably knew she'd had something to do with Lucid's meltdown, but she wasn't going to apologize. It was still performance time. She could maintain plausible deniability in Ryan's eyes.

"He's part of the universe," Raine said. "We all are." She held her chin above the shoulder of each grandparent as they stood up to hug her. "Congratulations on your anniversary, and happy birthday."

Raine met Lucid at the restroom door. His face was white and his eyes were red. He may have vomited. They definitely had to leave immediately. They'd made it through appetizers.

In the car, as expected, Lucid was still upset about what both Mom and Dad had said in such quick succession. He had both earbuds in now, but was being aggressive about his inwardness. Seething.

"Breathe in through your nose," Raine said, loud enough for him to hear. "Exhale through your mouth."

"I know how to breathe."

But do you?

"I should've helped more," Raine said. If her goal had been to keep him calm and for the family to have a nice time, then she'd failed. "I could've stopped them."

For the most part, Mom and Dad had both stepped up to keep the center of attention away from Lucid. But at a fiftieth anniversary dinner, it should've been the grandparents telling old stories of how they met and what Dad was like when he was a child, not about a middle-aged man on the verge of a psychotic break going for the feels, and doing it poorly.

Mom was just caught on the third rail between expressing

sympathy for Lucid and putting on her performance for everyone, Ryan in particular.

"I'm afraid Dad's about to have an episode," Raine said, trying to get Lucid to shift focus away from himself. "I fear he's been hiding his curse from Olivia and she won't recognize it or know what to do when it happens."

"He'll be fine."

"I'd like to believe that." Mom had always taken charge when Dad had his moments. Did Olivia have that in her?

"This is all your fault," Lucid said. "You made me go."

"Everybody wanted you there. You're one—"

"Did you tell Mom about Sydnee telling me my faults?"

That's right. That's what this meltdown was about. When Lucid was buried in his headphones, of course she'd told Mom about a woman being interested in him. It was big news. "One should never apologize for doing their best," Raine said.

"I trusted you."

They were silent the rest of the trip home, which was much quicker now with less traffic. She parked the car, and turned to Lucid. "Do you want me to lie on top of you? We can get the special pillows out."

He appeared to consider this. He rubbed his eyes. "It's okay. I'm all right tomorrow when I'm reborn."

CHAPTER
SEVENTEEN

17. WILLIAM

Geta had shown up at William's own parents' anniversary-birthday party. His parents, not hers. He knew there was a possibility she could show, but the idea hadn't bothered him until he actually saw her there. And now she was out-lasting the kids, who were her reason to be there.

William's parents had been saddened by the divorce. William wasn't sure how much those three had kept in contact since then, but of course they had. For the grandchildren.

He suspected the real reason Raine and Lucid had wanted to drive to the party separately was so they could leave early. Which they had. Lucid had made his much-needed appearance, and he was a built-in excuse for Raine's early exit. They'd executed their roles perfectly.

He heard Dad laugh at something Ryan said. He laughed so

easily. William wished he'd inherited that trait. It wasn't that William had no sense of humor at all, but he found he just didn't laugh much. Phil and his other coworkers would describe him as "dry." But Dad, he laughed while saying hello. Or goodbye. And everything in between was good-natured. Dad believed life shouldn't be stressful, and if it was, it was likely your own fault and you deserved it. And if it was truly someone else's fault, "Fuck 'em and have a toast in their name, anyway."

"Oh, look at that!" Dad said to the arrival of an order of Chateaubriand to the table. William preferred beef carpaccio, but this wasn't his party. And good on Dad for ordering what he wanted.

When William was little, Mom had told him you only need one really good friend and you're set for life. Lewis and Marian had been that for each other. But Geta was no longer William's best friend. He missed her. He'd like to ask Mom what would happen if you lost your one special lifelong friend to death or divorce. Maybe that's what sweet, unassuming Olivia was: the insurance friend who'd stepped in when William needed a new wife.

William ordered another drink. Olivia squeezed his hand to let him know to slow down. She was probably massively nervous being here, and needed him to navigate. She was the polar opposite of Mom. He needed to take the wheel for Olivia.

His parents and Ryan were talking about GMO food. Raine would've argued against it, maybe Lucid, too, but Ryan and Geta were proactive about it, that technicians could make food more nutritious and taste better.

"You can't bullshit a bullshitter," William interjected. "Splicing a gene from a fish into a tomato would make it taste like fish."

People's smiles were compliments. People liked the way he

thought. He was crazy and wacky and had the balls to say what was on his mind. Unlike Olivia, who would bite her tongue at the first sign of trouble. Sometimes he wished he could be a guest at his own party to see himself as host and entertainer. He never saw others as laughing at him. Why would they?

"They broke the mold when they made you," Ryan said. For example, the potential rival Ryan liked him.

"They sure did. But not before two of us were born," William said.

"Oh, here we go," Dad laughed.

"Not this again," Mom said.

William could tell by the look on Ryan's face he was confused. "I have a twin brother my parents wanted to keep me away from."

"William, stop," Geta said.

"Seriously," William said, talking to Ryan directly. "I saw him myself one day walking through a street fair. Exactly the same, like I was looking in a mirror. He was like Bigfoot, though, gone by the time you could get your phone out to take a picture." He was the only one who laughed, worse for laughing at his own joke.

"Thought you'd say your twin was blurry," Ryan said.

Everybody laughed at Ryan's wit, though.

Geta had brought a date. Sitting right there. Like bringing a boy home from school to meet the parents. To meet William's parents. To show him off. They were all smiles, and everybody liked Ryan. From what William was gathering, Ryan was older and more successful. Didn't travel for work as much, but when he did, he took Geta along. It seemed he spent far more time with her than William ever had.

William was remarried, so this shouldn't have bothered him. Olivia was sitting next to him, quiet and timid and unassuming. Saying little to nothing. He wanted to poke her with a finger to get a response. Do something.

But Ryan's presence did bother him.

He received a notification.

MOTE:

Even the Omnist loses numbers. Culling the herd.

THE PARENTS WERE WRAPPING things up on senior time, which meant by ten p.m., the time he was sometimes just leaving the office. It was too early; except for a round of golf on Monday, he hadn't been out in over a month, since the makeup birthday weekend he and Olivia had spent in San Juan Capistrano.

Outside the restaurant, Ryan and Geta were waiting for the valet.

"Come with us!" William said. "The bar's right over there." He intended to continue to charm Ryan over drinks so he'd stick up for William once Geta inevitably complained about him. And she would.

Geta and Ryan graciously bowed out, saying they had an early flight tomorrow, and William and Olivia walked to the other bar by themselves. It was a clear night; the concrete had absorbed the heat from the blistering afternoon, and warm air rose up from below them, while a soft crisp breeze hit their faces. Squished loquats, some dried flat, some fresh from a neighboring tree, were packed together so tightly in one section of sidewalk they had no choice but to walk over them.

"Ah-love-ya," William said, as he held open the door to the bar, as close to cloying flattery as he came, a mashup of "Olivia" and a sweet nothing.

This was the kind of place that, even though the floors

weren't sticky at the moment, you could tell they got that way sometimes. By the looks of it, most people were in their twenties, part of the unofficial gentrification program in this section of the Valley. Copious amounts of scented soap scrubs had been used on these bodies not an hour or two ago, and they were still kicking out their perfumes.

They found a couple empty seats at the bar that were mostly being used to order drinks over, not to sit in, so they sat in them. Olivia had had two drinks already, so she ordered a sparkling water. William looked over the scotch list before ordering one.

The Friday night voices were loud. While he was looking around the room, he didn't see or hear the bartender deliver their beverages. Men belly laughed, no inside voices. Women squealed. He figured most of the young men were either junior executives or trust fund babies. He didn't know why this bothered him so much, as Lucid was basically the latter, a child that didn't need to work. Maybe it was William's natural male competitive streak that had him so riled up.

"How about just one drink?" Olivia said. "I think I've got a headache from the sulfites."

"You think you're getting a headache, or you think it's sulfites?"

She didn't respond other than to avoid eye contact while sipping from her straw.

"You're feeling insecure because of all the aggressive, supple young women," William said. "I don't blame you for wanting to leave. Don't worry, I can still drive."

He wasn't the oldest male in the room, but she may have been the oldest female. No need to lay on that button. He swirled his scotch, watching its legs sweep the sides of the snifter. He always drank whiskey neat so he could do this. Ice ruined the body. Room temperature meant the scotch was alive and expanding. It breathed and interplayed with the air. And with your sinuses. Like Olivia, he didn't feel like talking. He would've felt different if Geta and Ryan had come. In retrospect, it was probably better they hadn't.

WHEN WILLIAM WAS TWELVE, they were all at Dad's friend Andy's house for a Memorial Day barbecue. It'd been a fine day. Music. Sodas. Tall tales. The sun had set and Mom was ready to leave. She was burnt out and grumpy. The kids were burnt out and grumpy. But Dad wanted to stay and talk and laugh and play cards on a folding table in the garage with the other dads. He cracked another beer and Mom threatened to walk the kids the two miles home. William recalled how forcefully Mom had grabbed his and his brother Bryan's hands and nearly yanked their arms out of their sockets.

Dad called for her to stop. When provoked, he had a manner of sounding stern and forceful while remaining jolly and smiling. It almost sounded like he was toasting everybody as he held his can aloft. "After this beer." he said. "Andy's telling me his camping story from last summer. Come listen."

"*One* more," Mom said, letting go of the children's hands. William wasn't sure if he was recalling his sense of time correctly, but that can didn't take long to drain, and Dad had cracked another and took a long drink. Andy was still recounting the story William remembered no details about. Mom, who'd wandered away to talk to others, came back and sidled up next to Dad. When he put his arm around her in solidarity, a fine, rapt audience for Andy, she smacked the new can out of his hands. It flew several feet and landed sideways on the ground, burping out its contents.

"I said *one* more!" Mom said. "Let's go!"

"On that note," Dad laughed. "It must be time to go."

It was a short drive, and the brothers were overtired and messing with each other in the backseat. William was the sleepier of the two, and Bryan kept giving him wet willies and poking at his ribs to annoy him.

They were at an intersection making a left turn when they got into an accident. Either Dad or the other driver went at the wrong time. It was nothing too serious. Everybody claimed to be injury-free, and after filing reports with a couple police officers, both cars were able to drive away with light damage. But something had happened to William. He'd bumped his head against the side window, and over the course of the next several days, his neck hurt, and he had headaches. Migraines, maybe.

Then he woke up dead. He felt as if no harm could come to him because all the harm that could possibly happen to him already had. He'd ended. Why shower? Why do chores? He plopped himself in front of the television. He didn't remember if he'd finished the last week of school. He probably hadn't. By the following week, he remembered doing family stuff again as if the Memorial Day fiasco had never happened. Under the rug, swept.

That had been his first episode.

WILLIAM ORDERED a second scotch and a glass of cabernet for Olivia. He saw a booth open up and they moved there, away from the crush of people ordering and spilling drinks.

"I don't want this," Olivia said, sliding the stemware away. He preferred that she complained about having another glass of wine in front of her, even if she didn't drink it, to his having another scotch. She would never slap a drink out of his hand.

As she sipped the wine, probably more out of boredom than anything, she looked sleepy. She was done for the night, unhappy, but quiet about it. When she lay her head on his shoulder and was clearly dozing, he tried not to wake her.

Before William knew it, it was last call. They'd closed down the bar.

He helped Olivia walk to the car. Once she was buckled in, she turned her head toward the door and fell back asleep. It was only going to be a ten- or twelve-minute drive home this time of night.

While making a left turn at a yellow light, an oncoming car accelerated to make or run the light. To avoid an accident, William accelerated to get ahead of it. The speeding car hit the back axle of their car and spun it around. The noise was earth-shattering. The airbags deployed. William heard his head crack against the driver's side window, causing a flash of light inside his head.

Then all went quiet except for the chime of one of the check engine alarms, a fan spinning somewhere, and escaping engine steam.

He envisioned himself rising above his unconscious body, and saw his wife still sleeping next to him. Her bag had deployed, too. He saw a bright, warm, friendly light, and floated toward it. Then he was sucked back into his body and he opened his eyes to find himself still in the car, in an uncomfortable position, looking directly at a streetlight through the cracked window. That must have been the light he'd been seeing. He couldn't remember what had happened, where he was, anything.

He got out of the car to find no one around. The other car had flipped over and steam was coming out of it. That wasn't a position a car should ever be in. It looked wrong; its underbelly was exposed like underwear. The streetlights were so bright he squinted and kept his head down. He didn't know where he was, but operated on autopilot, walking where his body wanted to go. Incessant ringing in his ears. He was only a few blocks from home, or he had little memory of a much longer walk. He found the front door locked. Of course it was. But his keys were still in the ignition of the wrecked car that he'd temporarily forgotten about. That's right, he'd left the scene of an accident. He'd deal with it tomorrow.

He went to the back door and found that locked, too. He picked up a ceramic turtle from the patio and smashed it through the laundry room window, clumsily brushed away the glass, and climbed through. He would get an email and a text of the video of himself doing that.

He didn't hurt in any acute sense, just felt unspecified body malaise. Physical ennui. Nothing felt right. He went to bed. He didn't sleep so much as lie catatonic on his back. He kept his eyes closed, as if he were an electronic item in sleep mode. No dreams. No blackness. No sense of time.

CHAPTER
EIGHTEEN

18. RAINE

The next morning, Raine knocked on Lucid's bedroom door. No answer. He was still in bed.

"Even cats are awake ten hours a day," she said. No answer. She knocked again. "You have to go to work, as well, dear Lucid." She knocked a third time. "I need to see you up before I can leave."

Lucid opened the door, climbed back in bed, but left the egg's lid open. "I need music," he said. "I need fresh blues and greens washing over me."

Lucid's collection of a couple hundred vinyl LPs took up the lower two shelves of a set of floor-to-ceiling bookshelves. He didn't follow sports, but there was an NHL hockey puck displayed on a little wire stand at eye level on one of the shelves.

He also had hundreds of books. Before he'd started

working at Omnist II, while Raine was at work, he'd read all day, play video games, or listen to records. Sometimes, if he could make it out of the apartment, he'd search for treasures in the used shops and flea markets he could walk to in Echo Park or Silver Lake. Even though their parents supplied him with spending money, he was good at finding bargains for books and LPs. Compared to others his age who were into snow-boarding or their cars or motorcycles, his hobbies weren't all that expensive.

"You must go to work," Raine said. "We ultimately have the same boss. This isn't like school."

"I know it's not like school." His hands were under the back of his head as if he were relaxed and contemplating, but his elbows were angled upward. He didn't seem all that relaxed.

The social aspects of school had been difficult for him. She'd expected more of the same at some point when he got a job in the adult world, so some of her speech was rehearsed. "Nobody's out to get you," she said. "No one's picking on you. No one wants to see you fail."

"Lucador does."

"He does *not* want you to fail. He hired you for your talents." Silence. He hadn't made eye contact since lying back on the bed. "I'll talk to him," she said.

"No, don't." He lifted his head. "He'll know. Then he'll pick harder."

"Don't quit so soon."

"I'm not quitting." He sat all the way up.

"Then don't get fired so soon. Make them earn it."

Lucid reacted as if she'd called his name. Devilish. She knew ending it on that note would inspire him.

She went to the kitchen and he shuffled after her, looking at his phone.

"Did you write this?" he asked, holding his phone for her to see.

MOTE:

Your soul is a muscle.

"IT SOUNDS LIKE YOU," Lucid said.

"Learning how your soul works is like learning a second language. Use it or lose it," Raine said. "And the muscle strengthens over time."

Raine began washing and cutting up peaches that she would put in bowls of yogurt for their breakfast. Rather than pepper him with questions about the anniversary-birthday party last night, a potential raw spot, she would let him speak as he was ready.

He wasn't exactly talkative, but every so often he would blurt out a few words he grabbed from the air. Sometimes, it snowed words over Lucid so much you'd think he had fifty choices for the word "falling" alone.

Some Lucid-specific vocabulary:

Bulwords. These were older, curmudgeonly stubborn words that moved slowly, stoically, like they owned the place and planned to stick around. These were obvious words, for example, those in the kitchen: cook, heat, rot, steam, cut, burn.

Flelling. This happened when words flew around indiscriminately like moths. Only words could flell, and this was a common action for them.

Mutables. These were unspeakable words he couldn't say. Once spoken, they disappeared, fading into oblivion. Mutables had as much right to be here as anybody else, so he felt bad when he spoke them by accident. This happened more often when he was young and had a smaller vocabulary. He could hear them in his head, but they were wounded if he so much as moved his lips as he read. Sometimes they were unpronounceable, which was a form of insurance for them to continue flelling. Most words weren't Mutables.

Obdurationals. This was a subset of Bulwords, mainly the nouns. Since they often had physical representations present in the room, like "refrigerator," they were less commonly airborne. The mass and gravity of an old, obstinate word and its object kept them near each other. Refrigerator-related verbs, like chill, cool, and spoil could flell farther away from an Obdurational like the word "refrigerator."

Lucid went back to his bedroom, and soon the sound of a Miles Davis record drifted out. One of his favorites. He was laughing when he walked back to the kitchen.

"What's so funny?" Raine said.

"I never noticed that play-on-words before."

There were no words in the song. "I wasn't talking?"

"The song. It's a play-on-notes, is that better? A musical pun."

This wasn't the first time Raine had caught him laughing while listening to jazz, but now she knew why: the notes cracked him up with their choice of colors and words.

"I like jazz because a saxophone can say words people can't," he said. "And they can produce colors only a careful listener can see. You get unique plays-on-notes with jazz."

Raine sat down at the table and sprinkled some trail mix into her peaches and yogurt. "Do words have souls?" she asked.

He didn't answer right away. Listening to the music.

"Like," she said, "if you lost a Mutable, would its soul go somewhere else and continue on existing, maybe as a new word, or would the word melt into darkness, into the vast nothingness forever?" She could tell he liked that question.

Lucid opened his mouth to speak, then stopped, still thinking. He did this again. "They deserve our sympathy and respect. Words are too often mistrusted, misused. We use them to create a shape of a soul for ourselves, but they themselves don't have souls."

Raine considered herself a dualist, like most Consumerians at Consumia's Spiritual Emporium. She believed in a soul, and that the soul would continue existing after death of the body.

Lucid, on the other hand, was a monist. It wasn't that he believed people had no soul at all—they weren't automatons —just that a soul was a creation of the body and brain, the soul thusly being intricately woven with how the brain worked. As people absorbed new words, new experiences, the soul changed, and upon death, was broken down back into its basic parts and reabsorbed into nature.

"Will you get ready for work now?" Raine said.

"I should rub myself with dirt and earth and let worms hang from my ears. That's already what they think of me."

"Your coworkers? No one will pick on you today."

"You don't know that," Lucid said. "Lucador might."

"Wash your face in a stream of consciousness." She knew he liked when she spoke like this. She thought about how they'd shaped each other's minds over the years. She'd certainly be a different person without her brother.

"I like this. A stream," Lucid said. "And words are fish, right? Salmon jumping up the river to spawn. To lay more eggs."

"Sure. And they live in water. Now go splash some on you."

"I'll shower now, for you, but I don't work until three."

Baby brother being baby brother. He could've told her that when she was waking him up. He must've wanted to share words with her before she left.

While Lucid was in the shower, Raine called Dad to see how he felt after last night. She was worried about him. No answer, but this was also not surprising. When he was busy, it sometimes took him days to call back. She imagined he would be pretty hungover today, but dutifully plugging away at his work deadline. He would've made a great stereotypical nuclear father in the fifties. Barbecue, Hawaiian shirt, khaki shorts, deck shoes. And hangovers.

A couple of his clients at work had played for the L.A. Kings, the local NHL team.

"These guys pay more in taxes than I make in a year," Dad, the humble braggart, had said once, years ago when they were all at a game. "And they should pay even more than they do, but we're good at our jobs." Maybe not so humble. Nobody in the family was a hockey fan, in particular, but Dad received a complimentary four-pack of Kings tickets every year, and they would go to Staples Center for a rare family night out.

"I like when the players shave ice to stop," Lucid said, drinking in all the sights and sounds. "It's a little blizzard that sprays over the words. That's what a snowstorm is; it's the gods playing hockey in the sky."

Raine and Lucid had rarely seen snow in person, just a couple times in the mountains.

"And the God of Words is the best player," Lucid went on. "He shaves the best ice. I've been in the biggest storms he made. The biggest you can ever imagine."

Maybe he had, maybe he hadn't, but it was his truth. "Even if you haven't," Raine said, "think it; it will happen."

A puck ricocheted off a stick at mid-ice, launching into the crowd. People around them stood up to catch it. It bounced off a hand in front of them and right into Lucid's grasp.

"That's my boy!" William said, toasting his beer at him, then toasting others around him who were standing and chittering excitedly at their near-miss.

Lucid shook his hand. But he wore a rare smile.

"Are you okay?" Raine said. "Did you hurt your hand?"

"Didn't hurt at all," he said, inspecting the puck while the two men behind him patted his shoulders. They didn't know not to touch him. "Like a snowflake landing on my tongue."

Raine had wondered if he'd seen and coaxed the word "puck" into his hands.

CHAPTER
NINETEEN

19. WILLIAM

William didn't feel rested. He hadn't slept, but just kept his eyes closed, not moving.

Thinking, not thinking. Remembering without memory of details. At least not at first. Memories were abstracted shapes pressed into his consciousness.

Then he snapped to lucid awareness. Most sober he'd ever felt in his life. His memories of "being sober" were often hangovers. Symptoms like headaches and grogginess were goals to overcome throughout the day until he felt almost normal. He should've been hungover today, but wasn't. This was different. He had no desire to have a drink, no hair of the dog, nor a coffee, or anything, really. Normally, he'd be considering ibuprofen and a glass of water right now. He was stiff. Everything was sore or numb, without acute pain.

He had two specific *"soberwhelming"* thoughts:

I am not me. He wasn't the same person he was when he woke up yesterday. That could be said about anybody, anytime, as people evolve daily, but he was now a stranger in his own body. Or he was the same person, but in a stranger's body. Whatever. Things weren't lining up correctly. But this shift in mindset was profound. The concept would've been unfathomable prior to this morning.

His second thought was: "Wow, everything is crystal clear. My memories, my thinking, my memories of thinking." All the hangover blurriness was gone; all the sharp edges, all the meanings and intentions of every conversation he'd ever had were clear. The present was everywhere. Listen to that leaf blower, the most temporary of a non-solution to a non-problem. He considered how people chased smaller numbers on a bathroom scale or on a golf course, then larger ones in bank accounts or video games. It was clear now how it was all irrelevant. The future and the past were the same, clear and useless, as if they didn't exist. Because they didn't. All that existed was an eternal, pointless present.

Throughout his adulthood, he'd chased goals that isolated him from the people he loved. Or from people he would've loved more, if he'd known them better. He'd really had no one to talk to these last four years since the divorce, about how dead he felt inside, episodes or no. He'd been wasting his life, and the lives of his family, by living this way. Actually, he hadn't really been living. He knew this now. It was now time to live the right way.

He sat up and, besides feeling stiff, was sensitive to sunlight. He shuffled out of the bedroom. No bathroom activities were necessary, but he looked in the mirror and saw his face crusted with blood. His nose was likely broken, but with a dial-tuning crunch, he straightened it out. His neck needed stretching, and he rolled his head around stiffly, but it wouldn't crack.

He reached into the shower and turned both knobs. He stepped out of his clothes and into the shower. The water was just right; no adjustments needed. He lifted his arms to rinse his hair and heard crunching in his shoulder. Every joint seemed to pop like he was driving on a gravel road. When he got out, he felt no need to dry himself with a towel. That would be unnatural.

He brushed his teeth and stared into his eyes in the mirror. His head was tilted a little to one side. It was like he'd slept on it wrong, the kink in the muscle pulling his head off-center. Instead of rolling his head again, he used both hands to twist it like he had his nose, and was able to straighten his neck with a celery-like crack.

His expression was bland, but there were no apparent veins in the whites of his eyes. He was more awake than he'd ever seen. He imagined this was what he'd look like if he went on one of those meditation retreats where you spent all your time in the lotus position. Maybe Raine was right. He needed yoga. *Feel like this, do this. Feel like that, do that.*

He wanted to talk to his kids and Geta. They needed to know he'd had these realizations. He wanted to tell Raine and Lucid how he agreed that none of the constructs of society mattered. Even less than they thought. They would understand him. He wanted to take them to a hockey game like he used to, and it wouldn't matter who won. Those goals scored were quickly forgotten anyway. Numbers were substitutions for real things. Surrogates. And he wanted the real thing.

He wanted to tell Geta he still loved her. He had chosen her, and she him. As cheesy as it sounded, it was life that had gotten in the way of, well, their life. He couldn't say why all this was happening. It was an epiphany that came to him while thinking-not-thinking. His ego, his cloudiness, his misdirection in life had all decomposed after that party last night.

Fuck. The party, the bar. He'd been in a car accident. He was married. His wife had been in the car. She hadn't been in bed with him. Where was she? He had to find her.

He searched through his pants, which were covered in blood, and found his wallet. His shirt was ruined as well, but these things didn't bother him. He had others. No phone; it was in the car. No keys; those were in the ignition.

He couldn't call anybody without his phone, as all the numbers were stored in there. Couldn't remember any phone numbers except his family's old landline from when he was a child. He couldn't even remember his current cell phone or office number. A number was merely a surrogate for the real thing.

Putting on clothes, he thought he looked halfway decent compared to when he first got out of bed. Didn't need to shave, still an acceptable level of a five o'clock shadow. Mostly, it was that his mind felt great, reducing life to a manageable set of achievable goals set squarely in the immediate present, not unlike those of a video game. Pants. Shoes. Short-sleeve golf button-up. Deodorant. Sunglasses.

First task: find car, find phone, find keys. He didn't lock the front door when he stepped out, just pulled it closed behind him. He walked through his treelined neighborhood, something he hadn't done since he first moved there. He had neighbors. Some had kids. Some washed cars in driveways, listening to music. His sense of smell, irritated by the perfumes in the shampoo, ached like his appendages did, like his chest. Like his head. Maybe things had always been this way, and he was just realizing it in his forties. Almost fifty.

But his vision. For some reason, it was crisp and vivid and loud.

He'd always claimed to have 20/20 vision. Better, even. Even while squinting in all directions. Geta and Lucid probably believed him. Raine enjoyed doubting him. She would challenge him, then relent and say the world was whatever way he thought it was. Now, his vision really was better. Widening his perceptual lenses created a longer "now," a longer present. His sight was a metaphor for encapsulating everything he could conceive.

The colors outside were aggressive, slapping him around, the light waves berating him like light sabers. Even though he couldn't look at the sun, he could feel the emanating waves. Both as straight vortices reaching out in all directions like sunbeams in a child's drawing, and as the concentric waves like that from a rock thrown in a pond. And the air was a prism, splitting the light into separate wavelengths, the colors of the rainbow. Most life on earth swam in the blue spectrum. The sky, the ocean. The sun was unrelenting and unforgiving, the source of all light, all colors, all life's energy.

Was this photosynthesis? Was he becoming a plant? If so, he'd be a mobile plant with self-awareness.

He arrived at the intersection from last night. Except for some glass swept to the sides of the road, there was no sign a car accident had occurred here. He began questioning whether it really happened. Some inconsequential stuff had occurred to some pointless material possessions. Insurance would be involved. Why should he care at all?

TWENTY

20. LUCADOR

It was three o'clock sharp, and Lucid wasn't there yet.

With Kick off today, Elijah was on the schedule. He could man the register while Lucador mostly worked in the Forgery. Lucador had sensed a reason to come out front, and was rewarded by seeing Sydnee there, browsing the aisles. Based on how much he'd seen her this week, she should know every item by heart. She smelled like powder. Or was it vanilla? Vanilla powder. He decided it was nice. Not for men, but for men to like.

Lucador stood next to Elijah in front of a display of swords, pretending to polish an expensive scimitar that didn't need it. "Which store do you like better, young Elijah?" he said, looking down to the tip of his sword, which happened to be pointing at Sydnee.

"I like this one because it challenges people's expectations," Elijah said. "You wouldn't expect to find this mix here. Games, alternative religions, organic food, hemp clothing, esports, LARPers..."

"My blades. They are the most popular of all!" Lucador had no inside voice; everything he said was the same volume. Loud. Which worked in his favor when he wanted Sydnee to overhear him.

"Great Omniscians almost every night," Elijah said.

"Almost?" Lucador couldn't tell how much Elijah was joking. They hadn't worked together enough. But for Lucador, incredulity was synonymous with strength. He liked being in charge, but preferred when Kick was around. He would never say that out loud, but Kick was sort of a leash for Lucador's personality. Lucador could be more aggressive when he trusted somebody was there to hold him back.

Lucador stepped away from Elijah and struck a Boar's Tooth defensive pose, in which he held the sword out before his right leg, ready for battle. Then he performed an Empty Fade, where he leapt backward with his feet still in-stance, then jumped back to his original position. It was a jerky video game move, but smoothness was an amateur ideal. The items attached to his belt rattled for a second after the move was completed. He liked that his jump had rustled up a scent of leather, oil, and sweat from his belts and sheaths.

"Are you sucking in your stomach to make your chest look bigger?" Elijah said.

"Oh, the Baby Kick," Lucador said. He patted his belly. "The baby kicks."

"I'm not a baby Kick."

Lucador didn't have a backlog of Elijah's personal information from which to tease, so he went for the low-hanging fruit. "You and Kick with the pubic hair on the face!" Both Elijah and

Kick had beards, although Elijah's was a new addition. "And you know I am right!"

Elijah rubbed his beard, shorter and more groomed than Kick's. Plus, Elijah was a twig. Two of him could fit inside Kick. Or Lucador.

Lucador raised a hand and cheesed a toothy smile at an imaginary crowd, a matador taking a victory pivot. He turned to see if Sydnee was looking at him. She was. "You'll come for my Lodge tomorrow, no?" he asked her, returning the scimitar to its rack. He'd wanted mannequins in fighting poses to display the best items, but Kick had said they were too expensive. Maybe at the end of summer. They could put them in fighting poses in the windows.

"Maybe," Sydnee said.

"My satchel, you don't have it with you?"

"Oh no, it's too...." After a moment, then, "But thank you, I love it."

Lucid finally walked in the door.

"You are late, young toro!" Lucador said.

It took him a moment to respond. Finding the words, maybe. "Bugs everywhere on the sidewalk," he said. "The bodies were dead, but the colors were alive. I stopped to count them. Three hundred and fourteen on my block."

"The bugs or the colors?" Lucador said.

Lucid cocked his head a few degrees to the side. "Both?"

"Hi, Lucid," Sydnee said. Her eyes were larger, rounder, when aimed at the boy. She should wear sunglasses.

Lucid didn't seem to hear her. That was good. This was Lucador's show.

"You missed the Cosmic Egg Omniscian last night! Perfect for you!" Lucador said. Lucid ducked under Lucador's attempt to ruffle his hair. "But never fear, Imani will return. The universe is vast, and it all came from the egg. Like you. Protective shell for growing. All the food you need inside. Grow up big and strong."

"Like those bugs...what if I'm not always safe in the shell?" Lucid said. "Eggs can break. They're too delicate."

"Make the fist!" Lucador raised his hand in victory. "You won't break!"

The kid was delicate, but tough. And he noticed Sydnee. "You have good words," Lucid said to her. "'Heal' and 'empathy.' Just like Raine has."

"Do you feel better today?" she said.

He nodded, looking at the floor. Then at her black boots. Probably embarrassed for fleeing the pretty woman the other night.

"Let's get you cheered up, Lucid," Lucador said. "Let's go in the back. I have something to show you. Come, Come!" They walked toward the Forgery, and before they arrived, Lucador ran ahead, rattling and clunking, so he could enter first.

"Olé!" Lucador belted, twisting himself into an awkward shape. He was trying to both dance and strike a matador's pose. He also hoped Sydnee would notice the chivalrous businessman, so good with children.

"What is this?" Lucid said. "A pile of junk?"

"It's yours! The Omnist Egg!" He raised a sheath from his side and tapped the entrance. "Enter there."

Lucid looked hesitant, but he got on all fours and eased himself into the crawl space to check it out. "Do you have a pillow?" he said.

"HaHAA! He likes! I'll get you a natural-fibers from the front. Two gifts!" He ran out to the main room to grab a pillow, making a "haHAA!" face at Sydnee as he passed, and when he returned, he handed the pillow into the crawl space for Lucid.

"I don't hear anything," Lucador said, cupping a palm to his ear. "That is good?"

A soft note of approval emerged from the tangle of wood and metal. Lucid had been astute; it did look like a scrap heap. But that was a good thing. Nobody would look for him there.

"What is that?" Sydnee said, standing at the entrance.

"It's the Omnist Egg! Ugliest egg I've ever seen." He lowered his head to the entrance. "But this isn't naptime, brave Lucid. Come on out!"

When Lucid emerged, he seemed to be in better spirits. Lucador gave him some in-store errands to do, which seemed to elevate his mood even more.

"Busy work is good work," Lucador said, slapping Lucid on the back as they re-entered the main room. Lucid didn't seem to appreciate the physical encouragement. "Idle hands are for making the swords!"

"Should I come back?" Sydnee said to Lucid, who was already distracted with the potions he needed to organize in the refrigerator. He didn't answer. She approached the counter to buy a kombucha. "What time does he go on break?"

"My Lodge starts at seven," Lucador said. "Good time to see the Lucid."

Sydnee left with a wave. "Bye, Lucid!" she sang. The front door jingled its own goodbye.

CANDLES SOLD WELL at Omnist II, which meant they went through a lot of heavy inventory. This was a good job for Lucid, moving them around and stocking shelves. Some candles were big, small, scented, and unscented; swirled, carved, and mixed with fruit peels, seeds, or other organic items; inside jars and glasses, or au naturel; they had dozens of styles. Some were intended for prayers, ambience, dinners, rituals, decoration, or even emergency light.

After unpacking and sorting, Lucador allowed Lucid to calculate retail prices for the candles based on bulk costs. Kick loved doing this, but Lucador hated it. Although Lucid's instinct was to price items low, for too little profit, he had no trouble crunching the numbers in his head. So Lucador changed the presentation and told him the percentage increase they required, and Lucid rattled off the numbers. While stocking the shelves, they played a word association game Lucador had created for Lucid.

"Red," Lucador said.

"Shel Silverstein," Lucid said.

"Why that name?" *Of course the boy thinks about shells.*

"Red sounds like read, r-e-a-d, and a book is meant to be read," Lucid said. "He wrote books."

"A twist of the words, a wordsmith." Lucador was rarely impressed with non-physical prowess. "Lucid's sword of words."

"And don't call me Sue," Lucid added.

"Loo-*Sid*. Not Sue." Lucador was tying little bits of canvas string to the story cards.

"Shel Silverstein also wrote the song, 'A Boy Named Sue.'"

"Ah, the young man-boy makes the non-funny joke!" Lucador said. "Let's keep going. How about...Rio Grande!"

"El Chapo."

"HaHAA! I know this one. A convict who escaped the prison multiple times."

"And the Rio Grande borders Mexico, and he's a Mexican drug lord."

Somehow, in the fraction of a second it took for Lucid to respond to a word, he could break it into pieces or determine an alternate meaning from which he associated a new word. The game had switched from Lucador testing Lucid how fast he could associate a word, to Lucid testing how fast Lucador could figure out what the association was. They did this for a while. Lucador was multilingual, but Lucid seemed to have a preternatural instinct for his one and only language.

"I know how you think," Lucador said. "Life is a movie playing in front of you on a giant screen, but you have another movie playing in your head on a smaller screen. You learn to watch both the movies at the same time."

"I guess," Lucid said. He looked sheepish.

"When we play, you find the words on both screens. That's why you need the shell. Shut off the big movie and chop up what's left so you can watch the words on the little screen. Can't find peace when two movies are playing!"

"That's not correct, but it isn't wrong, either."

"I like this; you chop up the words, you chop up the movies."

In this way, Lucid was an editor.

CHAPTER
TWENTY-ONE

21. WILLIAM

William stood on the corner he was positive the accident had been. But no car.

Next task: Find the wife. So William began the walk to the nearest hospital, Providence St. Joseph Medical Center in Burbank.

Traffic on the roads was heavy, the cars piloted by faceless, desireless, dead drivers. He didn't exactly feel sorry for them, as they were headed shopping, or to brunch, or to work. It was all just pointless. He'd spent hundreds—*thousands*—of nights working until eight or ten o'clock, and many weekends were consumed buried in the home office, ignoring his kids. And when he took a break, it was to play golf with clients or peers.

There was so much sunshine as he walked. Too much. He was wearing sunglasses and looking down, but sunlight bounced off the sidewalk and back into his eyes. Burbank had a lot of trees, but he realized how many more were needed to provide true pedestrian comfort. Keeping to the shade the best he could was helping; he wasn't sweating. His tongue and teeth were sticky, but he wasn't thirsty. He made sure to close his mouth. His old self of yesterday would've said this was a great day for golf.

His shoes were making a different sound than they had before. A scratchier noise. Off rhythm. He caught himself limping a bit from his sorer leg, and straightened up and walked like he was approaching a client in the office. Self-important and ego-driven. Things to do. Not projecting success meant you were projecting failure. These affectations, so familiar, felt fake and meaningless now. But he did them anyway. Some habits died hard.

He approached the front doors to the hospital. The shade of the awning meant the air underneath would be cooler, but he didn't feel it. It was difficult to tell. The automatic doors opened, and he was hit with a blast of processed air in which he could smell death. It wasn't unpleasant. It was the chemical tinge that bothered him. Made his sense of smell ache. He realized he could process smell better in this moment because the fans were blowing the air around, up and into his nostrils. The inside of his head needed to actually touch the air particles to absorb scents. Otherwise, his olfactory system was just sitting there, doing nothing. Somewhat dormant. Depending on the air currents, his sense of smell was working, not working. Like his consciousness had been earlier: awake, not awake.

The emergency room was filled, but wasn't it always? He kept his sunglasses on as he shuffled forward, trying to walk normally. He'd never felt that thing where you forgot how to walk or didn't know what to do with your hands when you felt you were being watched. And he'd never tried to avoid attention before, but was more self-aware and self-conscious than ever. All eyes were on him as he approached the desk.

There were few helpless feelings in the world quite like standing in line in an emergency room. Thank goodness he wasn't the one who needed help. He did, but only to find his wife. Some of these people were broken. He smelled death on a couple of them.

Over the years, he'd died so many times he should've acclimated to the feeling, and part of him wished this episode had the quality of invisibility with it, but Geta and Raine had always pointed out that they could see him. Invisibility was a dangerous symptom, as it could get him arrested. He didn't always remember what he said or did during episodes, but he wondered if he could in real time, like he was experiencing now. Yes, he must have. He did. It was later he forgot. Afterward, Geta and Raine would recount the events for him, and when patched together with details from his own spotty memory, he would create a sort of mosaic that someone not-himself did. It was almost like sleep-walking.

The receptionist processed what she saw. "Can I help you?" She was polished in her manner of speech in a different way than his help at the office was. Warmer. But still distant. Maybe more callused deep down.

"My wife," he said. But nothing came out. It sounded like he was choking. He pretended to clear his throat. Talking was odd. He had to expand his chest to vacuum air into his lungs, then squeeze it back out past his vocal cords to make the proper sound. He needed to be a wind factory. A fan.

"I'm looking for my wife," he said. A little better. He sounded raspy and broken. He should've practiced this outside before coming in. He blinked. His eyes wanted to stick closed, then stick open. This damn processed air. It'd been less of an issue outside. The lady may have thought he was flirting with her. He didn't have eyedrops on him.

"What's her name?" she said.

"Geta," he said. No, that wasn't her.

"I didn't hear that," she said. Concerned look.

What *was* her name? "Car accident. Last night."

She turned a page on a clipboard. She may not have been reading. Pretending. Then another employee, a nurse, walked up and they whispered to each other. Other patients in the waiting room were staring.

"Have you spoken to the police yet?" the nurse said.

It dawned on him he was the prey in this situation, and there would be more questions, stethoscopes, and needles coming soon. Perhaps a jail cell.

So he fled, moving as fast as his limp could take him out the doors. If everyone hadn't been looking, they certainly were now.

The receptionist yelled for him to wait. The nurse jogged around the desk to the automatic door like it was a property line she couldn't cross, calling for him to let them check him out, make sure he was okay. He moved past people and cars out front as fast as he could without drawing more unwanted attention.

He zigzagged his way home, in case he was being followed, then shifted back to walking normally when he realized how pointless that was. No one was following him. And assuming his wife was still alive, she would've told them who he was or where they lived. Or her driver's license would. Either way. She must be alive; he could feel it. She was at the hospital in a room or intensive care unit, and because he showed up there looking for her, the doctors would know he was alive now, too, and would tell her. In some ways, even though he didn't actually see her, something had been accomplished.

This new wife—the one in the hospital—she was nice. Didn't bother him much, didn't challenge him. All he'd wanted was a stable home so he could focus on the career. But that didn't matter anymore. Little had he known "till death do us part" meant waking up dead next to a someone so lifeless every morning. That was the last three years. She was a walking, sleeping, steady collection of relatively unflappable boring traits who deserved better than him. Both his wives had. He saw this now.

At least Geta had been *alive*. They didn't always agree, but she was independent and strong. She'd expected more from him. Demanded more. She couldn't be the only person in the relationship, she'd said. He now knew how much he'd been at fault; far more than the half needed for an attempt at reconciliation.

His skin felt weird when he got home. Itchy. He washed his hands and face and gargled a mouthful of water.

He hadn't eaten in about twenty-four hours, so he pored over the items in the kitchen and nothing jumped out at him. Dead people didn't eat, but no one was there, whether Geta, Raine, or his wife, to make sure he did. They would insist on it. He had no desire to cook or eat pre-cooked food.

He found the beef he was going to barbeque this weekend. Rather than fire up the grill, he sat down at the kitchen table and unwrapped the bloody package. He picked up the hunk with both hands like it was a sandwich and bit into it. He could taste the blood and iron a little bit. His sense of taste ached like his olfactory system did. Some juices ran down his chin and he sucked the blood off his fingers. Didn't really taste that much like blood. Wasn't the "blood" in packages of beef mostly water? Or food coloring or something. He hadn't cared previously. He did now.

He quickly bored of eating, not sure if his body was going

to accept the food. But at least he'd tried. He imagined sticking a metal straw into the cut of beef as a joke, but didn't.

He had no desire to watch television. No news feeds. Who cared about the economy, sports scores, political paranoia? Irrelevant. Besides calling his children and Geta, he wished he had his phone to see if he'd received any Motes that referred to this weirdness. If that was the word. He lay on his back on the couch and thought about thinking.

TIME WENT BY, because it grew dark outside. He had the urge to walk. He didn't turn on the lights in the house, or grab a jacket. He felt nocturnal.

He walked several blocks, hating the streetlights, cutting through unfenced lawns to avoid them. He wasn't about to climb fences. He was walking toward Griffith Park, where the roads would be closed off at night, and it would be darker. No people, no streetlights. But when a police crawler passed by, likely checking him out, he felt unsafe and headed home. A brightly lit jailcell would be hell. He straightened his neck and tried not to limp, self-conscious. His arms felt too straight. Then they flopped too much when he loosened them.

He arrived home and stopped just inside his door, standing in place. There was the random crystal clarity of certain memories or a sense of logic, which then faded back into a cloudy haze. Then his mind drifted back to other thoughts and no-thoughts. Some of his reasoning skills felt supernatural, but fleeting. As soon as he understood something about life or the universe, it receded. He saw the mess on the table. Somebody had left out a package of raw beef with a bite taken out of it. Flies were buzzing around. His wife was better than this.

When William was a teenager, the family believed there'd

been a poltergeist in the house. Things had moved during the night, sometimes making noise. He would wake up to find doors locked or unlocked, keys or wallets hidden. One night he was awakened by his mother while he was sleepwalking. He'd placed his baseball mitt under a cushion on the couch. Mom said he was trying and failing to get the cushion to lie flat. Her laughter had woken him. He'd been his own poltergeist.

If what he was experiencing now was a dream, he wished he'd awaken, so he went to bed. He lay on top of the covers. He felt exposed. He didn't want blankets, but the idea of his bed felt too expansive, too open.

He went back to his leather couch in the living room. He lay flat on his back, his hands at his sides, his feet up on the armrest. This was the right amount of space; he fit perfectly, the backrest reassuringly present on his left, and he wished there were three more sides like that. His feet had apparently been swelling from all the walking. He felt the pressure of the fluids in his body readjusting. He stared at the ceiling.

He heard a multitude of city noises, heard the streetlights pummeling him, wave after wave through the walls and windows, and he understood Lucid's desire to sleep in an egg. For William, though, it wasn't colors or words, but light. He heard too much light.

The LEDs of the entertainment center were mocking him, but he let this ride. A fly alit on his nose. He let this ride, too.

CHAPTER
TWENTY-TWO

22. LUCADOR

Lucador was with Lucid in the Forgery, cutting and preparing card stock for story cards to replace the incorrectly stamped ones out front.

"Question, young toro," Lucador said. "What color is the Omnist II today?"

Lucid looked at a card, considering. "Yellow? Maybe a sort of gold. There's no color word flelling."

"That is good!" Lucador said. "That'll do. Yellow is closer to the green than the red."

"The logos were green yesterday," Lucid said, rubbing the card stock in front of him. Lucador imagined it was the cards actually doing the rubbing. "They must've changed after I left." Who knew with him? Who knew what was going on in that pistolero mind of his?

"If that's the rule," Lucador said, "then they should change back to green when you return, no?"

Lucid had no response for this. He wouldn't press him. He wanted to, though. He was practicing patience with the boy; where was Kick to see this?

"Connie, she's good at making the stories," Lucador said. He was using a hole punch in the corner of the cards, then stamping a green logo on the front. "The idea for making the cards was hers, sí, but I have learned I am the best at it! I make the best stories! Tales! Journeys! Quests! We use bigger cards to fit all the words! People want to buy strength and victory and celebration!"

Lucid tilted his head sideways while he folded a card, like he was tucking a word into its bed. A flat bed. The cards were still blank inside, but who knew what he saw.

"Too delicate!" Lucador said. "Speed it up! Show the pulp who's in charge!"

He didn't speed it up. It was painful to watch how slow he was. But he seemed to care. "Some of these already have stories in them," Lucid said.

"They're blank! They're like the eggshells!" The cards were a bit more honey-colored and chunkier-looking than that, but no matter. "We'll write the words in later!"

"See?" Lucid held up an unfolded strip of paper. "It says this sword is for defeating mindsets of old."

"HaHAA!" Lucador raised his hands victoriously. "It knows! It already knows where it goes! And it is right!"

"If it already says that, do you think I should trace the letters so everyone else can see the words, too?"

"Good idea, young Lucid!"

Lucid wrote in the card while Lucador folded, stamped, and punched more of them. It was a better assembly line this way, anyway. An assembly line for the solo. Lucid finished his card and stroked the pulp lightly. He had good handwriting. He'd drawn each letter. Traced the shapes.

"I'll bring some blades tomorrow," Lucador said. "I know just the one the card wants!"

Lucid offered the card to Lucador, then withdrew it. Then he set it down on the table, but picked it up again. It was like he didn't want to let go of it. He was beginning to look stressed. "I don't feel safe here," he said.

"Never fear! We're the best friends now! I will protect you!" Lucador swung his arm toward the main room, clunking and rattling. "The safest store in Echo Park! The swords will protect you!"

Lucid went to the back exit and jiggled the handle. He looked like he was about to push his way out, but didn't. This taking care of Raine's baby brother thing was turning out to be harder than it looked. Thin ice. The boy could turn on a dime. Talented, but needed lots of handholding.

"You are safe," Lucador said. "Fire door. Always locks."

"I want my egg."

"Sí, sí. That's why I make the Omnist Egg! It's the best hiding spot! Best spot there is!" The semi-permanent junkpile, egg-casket-fort, was only a few feet away. "Climb inside. You've earned the break!"

This Lucid kid didn't show much gratitude. He just stared in a middle distance at the floor between them—not at the Omnist Egg, nor the back door, places Lucador expected him to flee. Lucid was a wordsmith who didn't use his words to show he was thankful. And the trouble Lucador had gone to for him. The lengths he climbed. The effort!

"It's called the *Cosmic* Egg," Lucid said. "That's where the universe came from."

"Sí! But this is the *Omnist Egg*!" Lucador said. "I made it with my own two hands! It lives here!" Still, the kid showed no respect. Lucid should climb inside like a cat in a box. "You owe me for building the Omnist Egg. I gave you a free office here... no, it's a bedroom!"

"But I don't want to live—"

"HaHAA! I know how you thank me! You take the stage with me tonight! Opening act! Show everyone how you pluck the words from the air, just like earlier!" He mimed picking fruit from a vine. "Like grapes!"

"It's not a parlor trick. I'm not—"

"Close the eyes. Let it flow. That's how I do it on the stage, I flow with the words, then I turn and attack the insubordinates that disobey! Keep them in line!"

"I never attack words," Lucid said, plainly and obviously, like he wasn't the weird one.

There was a knock on the doorframe to the Forgery. It was Sydnee, back again for tonight's Lodge. This time, she was carrying the leather satchel Lucador had given her. "Am I too early?" she said.

Lucador lifted a sheath from his side and tapped her bag with it. His bag. "The satchel of strength. That's more like it."

"Again, thank you. It's very handy. And beautiful."

"Was your exorcizing a success?"

"My exercising? I do work out, but—"

"No, lifting the weight of the spirits from the host!"

"Oh, yes, yes it was. And I brought Lucid a present." From the bag, she removed what looked like an antique nautical telescope in a brass mariner's casing and held it out. It was about ten inches long, in the tritone of green paint, brown leather, and dull brass. Lucador liked it immediately. "I made this myself," she said. "Well, not the original broken telescope."

Lucid walked over and accepted the gift without making

eye contact, putting it to his eye like he was looking for a faraway pirate ship.

"It's a kaleidoscope," she said. "Try using candle flame for light; it's fun. It flickers."

Lucid turned it slowly, then extended it a few inches and did it again. "My favorite." He aimed the scope at a work lamp in the corner. He shuffled backward until he was leaning against the Omnist Egg. It creaked. Would Lucador need to oil the joints? They weren't meant to move enough to make noise. "Colors everywhere. New patterns."

"I have a traveling gift shop I bring with me to festivals," Sydnee said. "I make lots of things, like this, and I have friends who make lots more."

"A Lucadorian attending the knife and hunting conventions," Lucador said. "I like this."

"Actually, they're more like celebrations in tune with the earth. All-night parties during full-moons and solstices with dancing, music, and bonfires. Lucid, you would like them. They're safe places for people like us."

"But Lucid sees the colors differently," Lucador said. "A gift of the protégé, a prodigy. A pistolero." He was both proud and annoyed with this turn of events from Sydnee. Conflicted. "You encourage him."

"Colors change as the earth's mood changes," Lucid said. "I see more reds in this than I thought I would, anywhere I aim. Many more reds."

"With this, your son will see the world in a beautiful tie-dye colorfast," Sydnee said to Lucador.

"He's my employee, my friend!" Lucador said. "Not my son!" *I told her this! Listen!* But seeing the world in ever-changing tie-dye patterns could be interesting. Lucid handed the kaleidoscope to Lucador, who immediately brought it to his eye. Fractal floral patterns of color. Very pretty. Fun for about five seconds. Boring. Useless. Looking through it would make your target more difficult to strike.

~

THE NO-BASIL ALCOVE at Omnist II was about a third to half full. Lucador and Kick had insisted on a good lighting rig for the performance area when designing the room. The multileveled stage was taller than CSE's, the first level about eighteen inches high, with a secondary plateau in the back, like a drum riser. The largest flatscreen in the house was on the wall behind the stage.

Lucid was looking through his kaleidoscope near the front door, possibly using passing car headlights as light sourcing. Sydnee was next to him, hovering as if they'd come together, and looking through a book of exorcism spells she'd just bought.

"Are you ready?" Lucador said, patting Lucid on the shoulder.

Lucid opened the eye not pressed to the kaleidoscope. He didn't seem nervous, nor engaged, nor enthused. But something in his expression said, "Don't touch me."

"It is time," Lucador said, then stepped up to the stage and spoke into the microphone. "HaHAA! Consumerians! Peoples! Lucadorians rejoice!" He raised a fist and some people applauded as they moved closer. "I am Lucador the First, but you already know that. It's my shop! HaHAA! And what a treat! Extra bonus show for you! A special worm for the early birds!"

He explained the rules of their association game, of which there weren't many, then gestured at Lucid. "And the star of the show, the Omnist Wonder, have you met him yet? No, he talks to no one, only me! But you will hear him talk! Lucid!

Come on up! Show everyone your face. Then we'll see your words!"

Lucid was frozen in a deer-in-the-headlights stare. Sydnee hooted and clapped, which encouraged others to politely applaud.

"Step away from the front door, young novillero!" Lucador said. "You might fall out!"

Lucid took a step toward him.

"Sí, sí, that's the way." Lucador descended the two steps on the side of the stage, walked over, and almost grabbed Lucid's arm. But remembering he didn't like being touched, Lucador swooshed him with two arms, like he could create enough wind to blow him the right direction.

It seemed to work. Lucid timidly ascended the steps, but once there, pointed himself at a forty-five-degree angle from directly facing the crowd. Good enough. Lucador left him like that.

"HaHAA! Sí!" Lucador could hardly contain his energy and did a lap around the stage, hugging the edges. He stopped in front of the boy. "Are you okay, Lucid?"

He didn't respond, but he wasn't fleeing or shutting it down, either.

"Time to play the game! You will be amazed! Everybody ready?" Lucador rubbed his thumbs against his fingertips, making the gesture for "cash." He was thinking. "I will think of a word, yes...how about...*beef!*"

Lucid didn't respond. The crowd was silent. Even with the door closed, traffic whooshed by outside.

"Come on, Lucid, it's the same game, the one we played earlier. Are you ready?" Lucador held a finger to his lips as if silencing the already quiet crowd. "The word is *beef!*"

Still nothing. Lucador unsheathed a sword and faced the

audience. Front guard. "I'll change it up for you. Let's get the blood flowing! The new word is *word!*"

Lucid was just a scared boy on stage. Time to be a man.

"It's okay, Lucid," Sydnee said. "Come on down."

"Speak!" Lucador said, raising his sword, conjuring all the power of the universe, all the words for the boy. This was the time. "Break the shell, Lucid! Break your shackles! The words!"

"Egg!" Lucid cried. "Shell, Eggs! Yolks!" He looked at Sydnee. "Horny! Virgin!"

"Grab the words, pistolero!"

"Can you see them, too?" Lucid was wide-eyed. Like a feral boy.

Channel the energy!

"I'll chop them!" Lucador held his sword like a bat, a batter waiting for a pitch. *Throw one here!*

Lucid reached out to snatch something from the air. "Guillotine!"

"HaHAA!" Lucador was happy. "Grass!" he said, swinging, hitting it back to the boy.

"Soldering iron," Lucid said.

"Dad!"

"Albert Camus."

Lucador lowered his sword. That was a word he didn't know. "Cah-moo? Like a camel? Or like a cow?"

Lucid was looking at the ground. He looked spent. "He's a writer, too."

"Sí, sí." Of course. The game wasn't as fun when Lucador wasn't catching the references. "You did good. We're done now." Lucador turned his sword upside down as if planting it into the stage. "Everyone, the great Lucid!"

The audience applauded politely, likely more confused than anything. Lucador wasn't really sure what just happened.

The game had been different. Less fun. Lucador bowed and gestured for Lucid to do so as well.

SURPRISINGLY, Lucid didn't spend any time in his Omnist Egg hiding place tonight. After Cara Pace's Lodge had begun, Lucador and Lucid leaned over the front counter, watching a cell phone video Elijah had taken of their short performance.

"What is that face?" Lucador said, referring to Lucid's expression. "You are not a boy; you are a man."

"I wanted my egg."

"Sí, sí, I knew that." But it was an overreaction. For a boy with who-knew-what going on in his head, he telegraphed fear too easily.

"A common mistake is thinking a turtle and its shell are separate," Cara Pace said from the stage. She was wearing a pulled cotton sort of faux fur, and just turning or raising an arm sent tiny snowflakes of dust motes into the spotlight. It was the opposite of wearing a shell. "They think the creature can leave its home for another one, like a hermit crab."

Lucador stopped the video and tapped the countertop with his finger. "Tell me, why did you say 'soldering iron' after the word 'grass'?"

Lucid looked at Sydnee first. She was standing over his shoulder listening. "You said 'grass' and grass is sod. I saw beads of silver grass, like dripping metal from a soldering iron."

Lucador could understand the soldering part, but he'd never seen grass as silver.

"But a turtle's shell is truly part of its whole," Cara Pace continued, projecting a well-rehearsed voice. "Inseparable. It's bone that grows outside the body."

Lucador backed up the video to rewatch the last few seconds. He stopped the video again. "After I said 'Dad,' why Alberto Cah-moo?" He wasn't sure how this was pronounced.

"He wrote *The Stranger*," Lucid said. "Did you read it?"

Lucador hadn't, but he wondered if the association meant Lucid thought of his father as a stranger. Absentee. Not close. Then again, Lucid was solitary in such a way everybody except his mother and Raine would probably be strangers. Lucador was a loner, too. No father growing up, so he developed the skills necessary to protect his mother.

"It's a wonderful book, Lucid," Sydnee said. "Existentialism on death row."

She'd read the book. This was a catastrophe. Lucador pulled Sydnee away by the elbow to talk.

"Use your natural protection," Cara Pace said. "Pull your head into your shell if you have to. But be prepared also to come out, to attack. Turtles do fight, and they are far more vicious than people realize."

"How old are you?" Lucador asked Sydnee.

"Twenty-eight." She crossed her arms, covering the logo on her shirt for a music festival dated five years ago. "Are you angry or something?"

"You know he's just turned twenty-one." He was a boy; Lucador was a man. She should see this. This was more than a catastrophe.

"I don't understand your implication here."

"He is the prey; you are the vulture!"

For the first time, he saw a different expression on her. She wasn't going to just accept what he said. She was a fighter. "Even if I was, he's not carrion. I would never do that to somebody. I was married to a violent predator. That was the dangerous situation, if you're looking to find one."

"I'm not afraid of your ex-husband," Lucador said, waving

his arm at the merchandise in the store. "I am surrounded by weapons, so many swords!"

"That's not the point. Lucid's an adult, and if you're not his dad, then stop acting like it."

"I am still his employer," Lucador said. "His friend. Yes, I am his friend. Why are you hunting the game?"

"Hunting the game?" Sydnee said.

"On the prowl. What do they call you, the mountain cat?" Lucador pulled his back straighter. He couldn't believe a Lucadorian was behaving this way. "No, it's the cougar! You're the cougar to his housecat!"

"I'd like to take Lucid for coffee and see if he's as crazy-wonderful and artistic as he seems to be."

"Do not call him crazy!" Lucador said this too quickly; he was too defensive. Because if Lucid was crazy, then Lucador was, too.

"I mean intense," she said.

Lucid was standing next to them. Lucador hadn't noticed him come over. "Insane works, too," Lucid said.

Sydnee looked embarrassed. "Lucid...I didn't..."

He didn't seem bothered by what they were talking about.

"You guys go now," Lucador said, lightly pushing them away. "We'll watch the video another time. You are clocked out. Get a coffee somewhere. Go chop up some colors."

"Actually," Lucid said, "I don't chop up the colors. They blend and bleed and run and swirl and..."

Sydnee took a few steps toward the door, looking to see if Lucid was following.

"Then chop the words and blend the colors," Lucador said to them as they walked away.

TWENTY-THREE

23. RAINE

Raine was home from work, and Lucid was at Omnist II. Dad still hadn't responded to her checking in on him this morning after his weirdness at the party last night. She was on the phone with Mom, pacing a sort of "Y" shape, starting in her bedroom, going down the hall past Lucid's door on the left and the bathroom on the right, then veering left at the fork into the kitchen. She'd reverse and veer down the other fork into the living room, then back down the hall again. She did this numerous times.

"He's not home from work yet?" Mom said. "I thought they'd be closed by ten."

"My wonderful sibling has made friends with Lucador and Kick," Raine said. "He's one of the guys now. Perhaps they're out getting a drink."

"He doesn't drink. You're okay with them forcing alcohol on your brother?"

"Mother, after all these years, you and Dad still don't understand him," Raine said. "Making friends is a good thing. I'm sure he's having a soda."

"You think I don't understand him? I give him money for rent and games and records. To give him the independence he needs. So does your Dad. He bought that egg-bed for him to hide in. And you think we don't understand? We're helping him. Helping *you*."

"You're enabling him to hide deeper. He'd like to disappear, and you seem to approve."

"And that's bad? Sometimes he needs to withdraw. You've said so yourself."

"That's true, but I mean..." Already known for speaking carefully, Raine needed to choose her words wisely. "You don't understand *why* he needs to withdraw. What's causing him pain."

"This is about the party, isn't it?" Mom said. "I'm sorry I told him he was features all the way down. I used the wrong words. But he is." She didn't sound sorry. She sounded prideful.

"You know that's not true. No one's perfect. And you treat him like he's a child and he might be smarter than all of us. If you say his faults are features, and he's features all the way down, then you're also saying he's all faults."

"I never said that."

"He knows what you mean even when you don't. He did the math."

Again, she wasn't a horrible mom, just not logical the way Lucid was. Raine understood his triggers better than anyone else.

AFTER ENDING the call with Mom, Raine made some herbal tea. Her phone buzzed with a text from Jacob: *How are you doing?*

The Earth thinks it's alone in the universe, even with all of us on it, she responded. *That's beautiful. But are you okay?*

She was so used to floating around the edges of other people's problems, she wasn't accustomed to people homing in on her own. *Sleep heals all wounds, then the sleep overrules.*

Seriously, don't do anything stupid! Will you pick up if I call? I'm referring to normal sleep, silly. I'm tired. Night, good.

RAINE WAS NEARLY asleep when Lucid came home, slamming the door with a bang, and stomping his feet louder than normal. It sounded like he threw his keys on the couch. She came out to the living room to find him kicking off his shoes, flipping them across the room. His hoodie was already on the couch. He was making loud noises, but as usual, he wasn't really doing any damage.

"Neighbors, Lucid!" she said in a loud whisper.

He shrugged. It was a little bit, *Oh, well,* and a little bit, *Sorry.* He was breathing heavily through his nose like was trying to self-regulate.

"What happened?" she said.

He didn't say anything right away. He usually didn't. But he was moving quicker than normal, too jittery.

"Did you have coffee?" she said.

"Maybe." He kicked his socked foot like a small child. There was nothing explicitly wrong with having caffeine, but she could tell he felt guilty about it. "Yeah. With Sydnee."

Raine sat down and patted the cushion on the couch. She

didn't say anything for a moment. They sat like this in the near-dark, the stove light from the kitchen and the nightlight from the bathroom providing most of the light. The light from the kitchen was whiter, bluer, colder than the softer sepia tone coming from the bathroom. The breath through his nose was whistling.

"Do you want me to turn the lamp on?" Raine said, finally. She always flipped on the lamp by the door when she came home after he'd gone to sleep.

"Darkness equalizes color," Lucid said.

It did. "Is it work?" She said this gently, in case work was now a trigger.

"No," he said. "Maybe." He was rocking a little. Not a lot, but it was like he was listening to a song quietly in head-phones. "Sort of."

"I told Lucador to go easier on you."

"Don't tell him that!" he said.

At any other job, having raw egg rubbed into your hair would qualify for a lawsuit. But Lucid hadn't been hired yet when it happened, and Lucid had sworn to her he wasn't bothered by it—it'd been her talking about his fascination with eggs that had been the problem. And now, asking Lucador to act like a proper manager was an issue, too. The irony was that both Lucador and Lucid didn't know how a proper manager behaved. They should look to Connie and Kick. Much better role models. She waited for him to speak again.

"They let me clock out before close, then Sydnee and I went to get coffee."

"That's great!" Now that she was thinking about it, this was eerily similar to how he acted the day he got hired. The hot-cold thing was how he handled good news-bad news.

"We talked for a long time. I didn't have much to say, so

she went first.," Lucid said. "She used to be married to a man that beat her."

"That's horrible," Raine said. She prided herself on understanding people, even their dark sides. She understood the frustrations that led to rapid heartrate, to cortisol spikes, but couldn't understand how someone could physically take it out on another human. Causing pain in someone else caused more pain for both parties.

"She cast protective spells, and tried to exorcise his demons while he was sleeping. He woke up really angry and hit her harder than ever before. That's when they got divorced and she became a Lucadorian. She still has a scar. She showed me."

"I can't even imagine," Raine said.

"And she's so kind," he said. "Understanding. But I could tell talking about it was helping. She had words like 'trust,' 'peaceful,' and 'placid.'"

"You're a good listener." Showing she was listening. This was his turn to be verbal.

"I told her how eggs can help her, too. How my bed is an egg, how all of life begins as an egg. Even her violent ex-husband started as an egg. Single cells are eggs. My egg-bed's in an egg-room in an egg-house. Eggs within eggs. A car is a traveling egg, a protective shell that moves valuables from one protective shell to another. People are valuable. Especially her."

Still, Raine wasn't quite sure why he was upset. The Sydnee story was startling and sad, but it shouldn't have affected Lucid directly. Not as much as his behavior seemed to suggest.

"She didn't want to tell me this at first, but then she did anyway: The kaleidoscope she made me used to be possessed, it—"

"Wait, what kaleidoscope?"

"Oh," Lucid said, brightening. He lifted the hoodie next to

him and there was something that looked like a nautical tele-scope underneath. He handed it to her. She couldn't see its colors well in the near-dark, but could tell there was shiny brass and worn leather involved.

"It used to be haunted by a mutinous pirate from two hundred years ago. She thinks he was murdered by the ship's crew, and then became trapped in the spyglass. He turned that to his advantage and ruined the captain's sense of direction, wrecking the ship on a reef."

"So, this is haunted?" Raine said. If true, she'd want to show it to Connie, Kat, and Dani, their resident medium.

"No, Sydnee exorcised it. Freed the soul. But I don't think it would've been all that helpful. The pirate's soul would've perished with his body."

Okay. So why was he frustrated? "Then what happened?"

"We were there for two hours, then Sydnee offered to drive me home. It wasn't that far; I could've easily walked, but she insisted. It was too late, she said."

Again. Sydnee seemed nice.

"Then after we buckled up, she said she was happy we were in the egg together!"

This seemed like a normal thing to say in Lucid's world. Sydnee had caught on fast. But Lucid seemed to be awaiting a different reaction from Raine.

"Don't you see?" he said. "Nobody's in the egg with me! No one! So I ran home!"

"That was sudden. It sounded like you guys were having a nice time. Did she touch you?"

"She did this when she was talking to me." He lightly set his hand on Raine's shoulder.

"Nobody likes being touched when they don't want it."

"No, Raine. I *want* her to touch me. But nobody is inside the egg with me."

"We're in a car together all the time."

"But not inside the egg."

"Not inside the egg," Raine said, nodding to show clarification. She'd always thought she was inside the egg. Maybe she was wrong. Raine got up to make tea again, and prepared one for Lucid, as well. She had a feeling they'd be up for a while. "You know, you're a fortunate soul."

"If you say I'm special and unique, I'll punch you in the sternum."

"Many people don't have somebody who wants to be in such close quarters with them."

"You mean the egg. I'd like to sit on the couch with Sydnee. Out here, though. Talk while hugging."

Raine gave him a look intended to say, "Please no further details."

"I find it impossible to date," she said, then realized she'd said too much. Wrong person to say this to.

"You?' Lucid said. "You're so pretty and amazing and... Do you like boys or girls?"

How had they never talked about this before? They must have. Maybe not. He had the gift of asking questions without them sounding loaded.

"I like beautiful souls," she said.

"Then why don't you date?"

She couldn't tell him. It would destroy him.

CHAPTER
TWENTY-FOUR

24. WILLIAM

The next morning, police were knocking at his door. Without a warrant they couldn't enter, so he waited them out. He found it easy to sit still and do nothing. Make no noise. Geta used to always win when they had a staring contest. Now he wasn't so sure she could.

The police went away.

Something new felt wrong. He'd already felt neither hot nor cold. Sleepy nor not sleepy. Hungry nor not hungry. But more so, now. Extra more so. He was extreme medium, an all-encompassing mood of oblivion. The everything nothingness.

He hadn't breathed since the knocking noise. That would tell most people what they needed to know, but this was different. He must have been respirating through his skin or eyes. It was a new level of meditation, one that would help his golf game, and he was guru of his own method. This probably wasn't healthy to do for long stretches of time, so he forced his diaphragm to inhale and exhale, but it was no longer automatic. But look, he was breathing. He felt dead inside, but wasn't dead on the outside.

He needed to start walking again. He put on sunglasses and a branded golf hat. He looked in his closet for more items to cover up from the sun. He put on a trench coat. He picked up a golf club. The weight felt good. He'd spent thousands of hours with a golf club in his hands. It was like a walking stick. It felt natural.

As he walked down the sidewalk, he felt he'd lost a lot of water weight, but his ankles were swollen and his stomach was bloated. He had gas. But he hadn't sweated or needed a restroom. It was evaporation. He was evaporating.

He thought about how Raine and Geta always called him out when he died overnight, that he wasn't really dead. That his condition was "only mental," they'd said. That his eyes were blinking, they'd said. That he still had a heartbeat, they'd said.

"This is just a postmortem spasm," he'd explained to them once, "What looks like breathing is just reflexive pressurized air adjustments. That doesn't mean I'm respirating." And he'd felt invisible.

This was different. No breath, except when he willed it. No blinking, unless he willed it. And people could see him, and they clearly knew something was wrong. A couple across the street were walking a pair of dogs down the sidewalk, the dogs pulling hard on their leashes toward him. The dogs weren't barking or growling; they just apparently wanted to come over and smell him, but the owners wouldn't allow it. He felt like a walking pork chop. But well-fed dogs didn't bark at dead meat.

Some people who walked past didn't look at him at all, which meant they'd noticed him more. Diverting their attention. Maybe he really was dead. He wondered if he killed a dog with the golf club, would it die and continue animation? Would it still want to smell him?

No morgue, though. No doctors. That wasn't the way he wanted to spend his last moments on earth. No more nights alone. Before he liquified, rotted into pieces, or turned into a leathery raisin, maybe he could enjoy one final night with family. The only people who mattered.

As the breeze shifted, he smelled rotten food, like that in a dumpster. The question was, from where? He thought of his throat like a tube to the stomach, and since he hadn't used a restroom in, what, thirty-six hours, maybe food was just sitting in there decomposing. His body's metabolism had stopped, but the bacteria were still feeding and multiplying. His throat was sticky and it opened and released a mouthful of gas, like pressure from a spoiled bottle of milk or orange juice.

He'd developed acid reflux after he turned forty, but this was an extreme version. It affected his entire esophagus, stomach, and intestines. Maybe even his mouth. He'd heard humans described as merely bags of digestive bacteria and enzymes. Bags with holes at the top and bottom. With legs and arms to put biomass fuel into the bag. But now, he was experiencing it. His shape was temporary. Was he more bacteria than human? Had he always been?

He felt like he was digesting his own teeth.

The bacteria were going to win.

Walking didn't feel good, didn't not feel good. He just didn't want to sit around and rot by himself. Carrying a golf club gave him a better sense of balance. It lowered and spread out his center of gravity. He walked through the mist of an errant lawn sprinkler that was spraying over the sidewalk. Water mist condensed on his hand. He held it up to look at the tiny droplets of water, tiny little worlds, tiny little eyes that viewed the world the way he did. Through little bubble lenses. He wished he could look out through the droplets.

William stopped at a drugstore, and when the automatic doors opened, an older lady stopped dead in her tracks. She looked him up and down, then stared at the golf club. He didn't need it, so he leaned it against a trash bin outside the doors. He could smell something organic rotting in the can, which, now that he thought of it, was an exposed stomach with only one hole—at the top. The smell didn't bother him like it used to.

As the woman walked past, he heard her say under her breath, "Drunk."

He probably looked intoxicated. That was preferrable to looking dead. He'd done this many times before, trying to seem normal to others after he'd died. He went inside the store. He wanted a bottle of antacid, something to neutralize the rotten gases in his stomach. He struggled trying to decide which antacid he could get down his throat and keep down, whether in drinkable or chewable form. He would buy one of each. He also grabbed a bottle of eyedrops.

Standing in line, he felt like he looked homeless. Like his clothes were old and dirty. He caught the image of himself in the security monitor, and when he straightened up, he looked like any other customer that hadn't slept the last two nights. He ran his fingers through his short, thinning hair, his shoulder crunching. He reminded himself to blink. Sticky and gooey. His lids were catching, but he was mere moments away from receiving eyedrops.

The lady in front of him kept turning to look at him. Did

she smell decomposing food? He closed his mouth and made a grumpy noise like he was clearing his throat. It vibrated like a garbage disposal. It wasn't his voice.

At least the purchase on the card was small enough he didn't have to test his dexterity signing anything. He waved off needing a bag. He had pockets in his trench coat.

Once outside the doors, he struggled with the child-proofing on the bottle of antacid and popped in a chewable pink wafer. He moved his jaw up and down mechanically, like he had seen others do. He'd forgotten how to chew. The instinct was gone. His mouth was stale, gummy, and he couldn't swallow. He opened the liquid version of antacid and tried to use it to wash down the crumbled and mushy pill.

Maybe one swallow made it down his pipe. The rest was spit out like pink vomit.

Putting in eyedrops was an adventure. A lot of his coordination was gone—not like using an eyedropper had ever become muscle memory or anything—and when he was done, his cheeks were dripping wet like he'd been crying.

Now what. Boredom was the wrong word for this feeling. Pretending nothing was wrong was closer to the truth, but was there a name for it? He walked again, switching to the more shaded side of the street. As he passed a sushi restaurant that was just opening, he decided to stop for lunch.

"Inside or out?" said a hostess, holding a menu at a kiosk on the sidewalk.

Rather than try to speak, he pointed at a shaded outdoor table. Indoor seating was out of the question, as he was concerned others could smell him. He sat down, the chair's aluminum legs scratching and rumbling across the concrete, sounding like he felt. His eyesight was still clear when he looked at the menu, but like in dreams, the letters seemed to swim around into nonsense arrangements. He scratched the corner of his mouth and saw pink on his nail. He'd been walking around with antacid crusties on his mouth.

He still wasn't thirsty, but the server put a glass of ice water on the table. He sipped and swished the water around to refresh his mouth, then when nobody was looking, spit it out on the concrete behind him. More eyedrops.

He ordered sashimi. An order each of tuna and salmon. It wasn't much, but all sushi restaurants had this and he could do it without deciphering the menu.

Even without an appetite, he didn't want to go too long without food. Blood sugar or something. His brain was already swimming. He swallowed a sip of water when he was done eating to make sure the raw fish had gone down. The fish was bland, unexciting, really. If anything, it nauseated him.

He started to get up, struggling with an apparently weakened back. He realized he may never eat again. The server rushed out to bring him his check. He would've accidentally left without paying.

Signing his bill, his handwriting wasn't his. His signature had been illegible since college, but it was almost exactly the same each time he scribbled it, and it was nearly unforgeable. But even he didn't recognize it anymore. It looked like someone had been holding the pen like a club and raked it across the paper. Which was basically what he'd done.

He needed to find somebody, anybody who would understand what was happening to him. That's right. Final night. Spend it with family. So he'd walk to Consumia's Spiritual Emporium, where Raine worked. She knew random weird stuff about people and science. And she was familiar with his curse.

This walk was longer than his treks to the accident site, hospital, or restaurant had been. More sun. More absence of sweat. The sun changed places in the sky. Shadows elongated.

He was hoping Linden Vowel would be there. He was the

host of Coffin Club, and he taught wood shop at a local school. A few months ago, William had asked him to make Lucid an egg-shaped coffin-bed for his twenty-first birthday. Some kids wanted a case of beer or a bottle of liquor, a night on the town for that milestone. Las Vegas. Lucid didn't.

"That's rather morbid for a gift," Linden had said, jovially, and William wasn't quite sure if he was being mocked.

"Coming from the guy who wants you to buy a coffin for fun," William said.

"A box is for decorating. It's personal. You intend this as a toy. A box isn't a plaything."

"No, no, he won't be disrespectful with it. It's so he can sleep in it."

"A teenager alone in his bed?" Linden lifted his eyebrows, which lifted his entire face.

"Ha," William said. "I see what you did there."

Raine had entered the room, and Linden asked her if this gift was for real. She said it was, of course. "Only a soul so full of life could desire something as macabre to sleep in as a coffin," she said. That had clinched it.

Linden made the egg-shaped box. It was easily the size of two coffins, nearly wide as a twin bed, and taller than a coffin, like one stacked on top of the other. He'd refused to accept money for it. "It's for Raine's brother. My gift to him."

William couldn't allow the gift to be from Linden, so they compromised with William at least covering the cost of materials. It was his idea, and he wanted credit for thinking of it.

WILLIAM CURRENTLY ENTERED CSE. Spices, oils, incense, amber, musk: The smells were pleasant, but dull, achy, and earthy.

Dusty and alive with death. Like a living tomb. Even his vision had darkened a notch. Like looking through an amber lens. The edges of his vision were blurry.

As he stood in an aisle, a customer brushed past him, kicking up air, swirling it around him. William smelled decaying flesh, like roadkill. Maybe it was the beef from yesterday rotting in his teeth or stomach. He opened his mouth wide, like he was stretching his jaw muscles, and gas released from his throat again. The antacid hadn't done much. He had to keep his mouth closed.

The cashier had black hair with bleached bangs, a black pencil skirt, and black T-shirt with the image of a fried egg representing the Milky Way. The Milky Way as an egg would've seemed humorous a few days ago, but now made as much sense as anything else, if it even mattered. She looked like an alternative model who'd come straight from a photo shoot. He picked out some local organic breath mints in a retro-styled tin and set them on the counter.

"Kat," said Raine, poking her head out of the office in back. "You've met my father."

Right. He'd met Kat before. She slid the mints back, looking at him oddly. "You're good," she said.

Good? He wanted to say, "I don't know about that," but forcing out air and hoping his vocal cords and mouth made the intended sounds felt like too much risk. It felt like Kat was barely refraining from stabbing him with a wooden stake.

He nodded approval. Kat kept staring as he limped over to the Basil Alcove to wait for Raine. He put a mint in his mouth, tried to suck on it, and immediately gagged and spit it out, the mint landing near one of the points of a giant pentacle painted on the floor for Lodges and rituals. The sound was both loud and muffled, as if he were an insect on the floor next to where it landed. Way louder than it should have been. Also, he noticed an otherwise lack in hearing middle frequencies. He heard more high-end frequencies than before, like his blood pressure had been previously obscuring them. Without that ringing, these sounds filled the gap. He also felt deeper, low-end sounds through his body.

He kicked the mint away with his foot. Away from blame. He almost slipped. Sitting down at a table would mean getting back up with watchful eyes around. The message on a black poster took him a moment to work out, one spinning word at a time. It was a quote from the Omniscian Yksian:

I ONLY ALIENATE two groups of people: those who believe in God, and those who don't.

SOUNDED LIKE A MOTE. If only William had his phone.

"Dad," Raine said, suddenly behind him. She was the quietest walker he'd ever met. A jolt of excitement shot through him. "You look like a willow tree suffering a drought."

It was obvious she could tell something was wrong. *It's okay, this is my daughter.*

"Ugh." He was thinking with more words than what was coming out. He wanted to say he missed her, missed Lucid, missed Geta. He practiced a few breaths, tried working his tongue around his mouth.

"What's wrong with your neck?" she said.

"Golf injury." Mouth full of marbles. He roughly rubbed the side of his neck.

"Cramped muscle?" she said.

He nodded a little. His vertebrae made popping noises in his head.

"You don't look healthy. I'm worried about your diet. Are you sleeping? Is your nose broken?"

Multiple questions at once crashed his system. He shut off again. His default mode was nothingness. Conversations moved too fast. This was CSE, right? Why was he here again?

"Let me tell Connie I'm going on break." Raine went to the back office for a moment, then escorted William into the Dark Arts room.

No Linden Vowel present. But it was an appropriate room for a man who was dead. The critters in formaldehyde were mocking him. He wondered if he would stop his internal putrefaction if he drank some. It had to be better than the antacid. Slowly, he worked his chest and mouth muscles best he could.

"Let me drive you to the hospital," Raine said.

"Already been." Why was he here again? "Need to see my son."

This seemed to trigger something in Raine. "Lucid's at work. I'll drive you."

They exited out the back door and walked to where Raine had parked.

"Am I dead?" he said once they were seated.

"Buckle," she said.

As if it mattered. He buckled his seat belt anyway.

"The real question is, 'Are we alive?'" she said.

"No." His voice was dry. "Am I dead."

"Ninety-nine percent of what we see of each other is dead, so yes, you look deceased."

This wasn't working, because he'd been "dead" to her before. Many times. But he'd always been alive, just thinking he was dead. Maybe he was doing it again. He had to trust her.

"Dad, I don't even believe you have Cotard's delusion. That only afflicts, like, two people per billion."

"Never claimed that."

"Think about how all of life is a mental projection. That means, by definition, we're all delusional. But you take it a step further. It's like you have a delusion about having Cotard's delusion."

TWENTY-FIVE

25. RAINE

"Where are we going?" Dad asked with more vowels than consonants.

"To see Lucid, remember?" Raine said.

Dad was having trouble with his memory. He looked like he'd slept in the street, if he'd slept at all. He must've walked all the way from his house, several miles. He'd probably fallen and hit his nose, cramped his neck. If she didn't know better, she'd think he'd been on a bender since the party. Raine wasn't sure Olivia even knew how to deal with one of his episodes. But if he wanted to see Lucid, he could. It was the least she could do. When Dad was like this, the kids could talk to him better than anyone else.

She battled internally about whether she should play something to distract him. Then again, did somebody staring straight ahead, not moving, not even blinking, really need a distraction? He'd gotten better at this faking-dead thing over the years. Sometimes she thought he was joking when he did this. An extremely not-funny joke.

"Are you okay, Dad?" she said.

"You're right. I'm alive."

He never gave in that easily. "Only living people can have Cotard's delusion," she said. "You said an old golf injury is flaring up."

"Golf," he said.

"Only living people play golf."

"Pointless." He showed no emotion. If he were holding a television remote, he'd mindlessly flip stations, not focusing on any one show. Other things stuck out to her, like how he didn't initially put on his seat belt. Or that he was wearing a warm coat, hat, and sunglasses on a hot day. Maybe he was hurting too much. Heat was good for keeping muscles loose.

"It's so clear," he said. "I'm here. You're here."

"We *are*, and we are everything," Raine said. "Have you spoken with Olivia?"

"Who?"

"Your wife."

"Your mom, good. Came to party."

"No, your wife, *Olivia*."

He'd forgotten about his wife. This was upsetting.

"Everything is now," he said. "She's okay now."

Tora, the Power-of-the-Present Omniscian at CSE, may have some thoughts about this, because to Raine, what he was saying didn't make much sense.

"Take me to son," he said. "He understands."

"His name is Lucid."

"Family. Sleep on couch?"

He'll be fine tomorrow. These episodes never lasted more

than a day or two, but this was definitely a bad one. Raine would call Olivia after she dropped him off with Lucid and let her know Dad was going to spend the night with them.

His stench was palpable. He smelled like a dumpster on trash day after the food had had a couple days to ferment in the sun. She'd been correct when predicting at the party he'd soon have an episode. "Sure, Dad. You should take a shower and sleep it off."

When Raine was in high school, a few years after Dad's Santa Barbara incident, he'd had another episode and thought he was dead again.

"Hi, Dad," Raine had said when he walked into the living room.

"Oh, I'm surprised you can see me." Dad looked around to see if anyone else there. "I wore clothes out of respect. So you *can* see me."

"Of course I can."

"But you're just seeing my clothes, not me."

He said he'd been craving beef carpaccio because, well, of food that living people ate, he believed the undead would eat it. He insisted on going to dinner at a nice restaurant that served it. He leaned over to whisper to Mom.

"Why don't you order it yourself?" Mom said.

He whispered again, but Raine heard his answer this time. "The staff shouldn't talk to the dead. It's probably a bad omen."

On some level, he had to know he was being foolish.

They took him to the doctor from the restaurant. It'd turned out that dinner was a negotiation tactic Mom had employed that evening to convince him to leave the house. When Mom asked the doctor if Dad was healthy, if maybe he'd had a stroke or something, she'd said he was physically fine. Needed rest, a break from work. A break from problems.

Because when it came to problems, Dad never admitted to the major ones, but often complained about the minor ones. He'd bought a new car once because he wanted a better cup holder, but then he'd never talk about their finances.

Raine had always tried to be patient with him, to let him live his journey, follow his own path. This seemed different, though. This episode was more thorough, like he'd prepared more. She imagined him rubbing kimchi and dumping unsweetened kombucha all over his body before getting dressed so he would smell like death.

"Past, present, future," Dad said, perking up somewhat. "Soul aches. Diminishing." He touched his cheeks and forehead like he'd never felt them before, like he was blind and learning a stranger's features.

"All life breathes as one," Raine said.

"Wet air. Bacteria."

This didn't sound like hypochondria this time. The descriptions were too much what she'd expect from someone who was actually dead.

"Within you lies the power to heal yourself." She wished she could see what words were flelling around him, the way Lucid could. She would grab the necessary ones to help Dad.

They arrived at Omnist II. Since Lucid had started working there, and he was a bit of a wild card, Connie and Kick wanted Raine to have a key, as well, for Lucid's sake. Raine and Dad went in through the back to avoid attention. She sat Dad down at one of Lucador's work tables in the Forgery. Lucador had been detailing a sword that was resting on the table near a gas-powered desktop forge. Dad slowly stroked the groove in the middle of the blade like it was a cat lying in the sun.

Raine went to the front of the store to tell Lucador about Dad's presence and retrieve Lucid. "Can you accompany him in his journey for a few hours?" she said.

Lucid didn't otherwise acknowledge her, but walked with her to the Forgery. "Pasty and brown," he said when he saw Dad.

Dad did look pasty, but not brown. A bloodless face. There were unscabbed pink pock marks like he'd been scratching himself.

"He's having another episode," Raine said.

"Still alive." Dad wasn't bothering to make eye contact as he spoke. "Still here."

"He's learned to accept he's suffering a delusion, but as you can tell, he's no longer aromatically enhancing with deodorant or aftershave."

As if this were the deciding factor, Lucid nodded.

"He's been asking to see you," Raine said. "And he wants to stay the night with us. I'll call Olivia on my way back to CSE."

OLIVIA'S CELL went straight to voicemail and Raine left a message. She was probably working in her garden.

Fitting that tonight's CSE Lodge was hosted by Amelio, an Omniscian who specialized in healing stones, tinctures, and prayers. Raine couldn't stop thinking about Dad as Amelio took the stage.

"Hi, Consumerians, I'm Amelio. Not Amelia or Emilio, which are both fine names, but *Amelio*. Starting with an 'A.' Some people call me 'Doctor Nurse.'" They'd had some work done on their face. It was difficult to tell how much of their smile was natural, a person who was constantly smiling, even when alone, and how much was from tightening the skin on their face. They were older, possibly in their seventies, but walked like they were decades younger. Sneakers, sensible white shoes.

"When you heal the mind, you heal the body. Heal the body, heal the mind. Both are equally important, and should never be done in isolation."

Amelio sold healing stones of many colors, all polished smooth and perfect to rub in your hand while listening. Some held heat far longer than others, which made them ideal to place at specific points on the body. The herbal tinctures were formulated to put in their branded Amelio-Air humidifiers, a big seller in the Valley, where the concept of dry earned its name for at least six months every year. They sold more than fifty different concoctions—half medicinal, half spell, really—to assuage a wide range of symptoms, from anxiety to weight gain, infertility to sleeplessness. But most were healing tinctures that focused on a single bodily issue: the head, back, skin, eyes, nose, or throat. Digestion. Lactation. Blood pressure. Soreness.

"There's a lot of talk about the seven stages of grief, as if they're steps you have to take in order, one at a time," Amelio said. "But this isn't true. The stages exist, yes, but the order is different for everyone, and setbacks happen. One day you've found acceptance, the next it's gone. But this is normal and okay. And if you've lost a loved one, then another, like losing a second or third parent, as I have, it's different each time. You're a different person each time you go through it."

Raine wondered what stage of grief Dad was going through to be that disconnected with reality. What was he escaping?

"God, or Source, or whatever higher power you ascribe to, they are a nurturing, healing entity," Amelio said. "They want you to heal yourself, to heal the world. To heal the healers."

Raine bought a few of Amelio's healing stones. Her new favorite was a deep green malachite, a copper carbonite with black striations. A healing stone that protected against negative energy, it was polished so silky smooth that the green color seemed to spill past its edges. It fit so perfectly in the palm of her hand, she'd think that's where it was formed. She wanted to rub it between her palms, the fingers of one hand turned at a ninety-degree angle from the other. Lucid would love this.

And she bought a healing tincture for the humidifier. Dad often complained about the dry air, and there was an entire summer ahead of them. He'd appreciate this tonight. Plus, maybe it'd help him heal.

Now that she thought of it, maybe Raine should've kept Dad here at CSE to listen to Amelio, instead of leaving him at Omnist II, in the vicinity of Lucador.

TWENTY-SIX

26. LUCADOR

William Oxford was currently in the Omnist II Forgery. Father of the two strangest employees of the vast Omnist empire, William the First was royalty. William was a stand-up soldier. A businessman's businessman. Would be great to have a tequila with and talk shop—talk about the new venture and its problems and successes—and William could thank Lucador for his great work with Lucid. Lucador was now both a second dad and a second sibling to the boy. Lucador had met William a couple times at Consumia's Spiritual Emporium, but he hadn't seen him since Omnist II opened.

"HaHAA!" Lucador said, cheering away a couple departing customers who were laughing at his effervescent enthusiasm.

They obviously recognized and appreciated Lucador's star qualities. This was the break in the action Lucador was looking for, and he patted the counter to beckon Lucid over like a puppy. Lucid didn't know how to use the registers yet, but he could send inquisitive customers to the right shelves. Lucador retreated to the Forgery. "The infamous Lord William of Oxford!" he said as he entered the room.

"Air is syrup." William was petting an unfinished sword. "Blade?"

Lucador repeated what William had said three times in his head to make sure he'd heard him correctly. A Raine observation if he ever heard one. Maybe William was asking for a sword to cut syrupy air. A butter knife for the jam?

"You pet it like a pet!" Lucador said, taking the sword from William and watching his face follow, a little behind the movement. Odd. Maybe William was drunk. Garbled words and slow reflexes. That's why Raine brought him here. To dry him up. He set the sword on a stack of boxes. "Do not move! I'll be back!"

Lucador went to the front of the store to retrieve a cup of the iced tea blend from the cistern at the end of the counter. Lucid was watching a screen of a first-person shooter game blowing away attacking zombies. *Wimps! Anyone can use an automatic rifle! Swords! That's the real skill!* When Lucador returned to the back, it looked like William hadn't moved at all. He'd been good at taking direction, was perfectly still, staring at nothing.

"The meditation king, too!" Lucador said. This man was really something. William didn't reach out to accept the cup, so Lucador set it on the table.

"Blades cut air," William said.

That was his cue. Lucador picked up the sword again and

began lunging and striking an invisible enemy, the way he'd demonstrated for his students in the classes he taught at the park. "William, the formidable Oxford," he said. "You should attend my class. I'll teach you to cut the air! And when needed, your enemy, too! HaHAA!"

"Mucus. Lungs, eyes, air. Store is mucus."

Nobody calls Omnist II mucus, even if William is speaking through a mucus pillow.

"I'll make you a machete, maybe," Lucador said. Those were less about being sharp, but more about the mass, the force, to obliterate your way through anything. Nothing wrong with using a little back, shoulder, and arm strength. Most people forgot about the power generated from their hips. Good torque. "You're a golfer, William, so you would know about using the hips! Like this!" Maybe Lucador would add a fuller to the blade to reduce suction, the stickiness of William's enemy air.

"Years in a day," William said. "Sleep, pointless."

He liked how William was talking. Like Lucid, but with the added wisdom of years. Short sentences, to the point. "Four and a half hours a night!" Lucador said. "That's all the warrior needs!"

Who cared if William was wearing a coat on a hot day? Big deal. And a hat and sunglasses. Like the invisible man. Maybe this was where Lucid inherited his desire to hide, to be invisible.

"I am honored you are here for my Lodge, William...Dad." Even though Lucador was nearly William's age, he was still at least five years younger, and he meant the comment with utmost respect.

William didn't answer, just sat staring. Something was definitely wrong.

"I'll get the Lucid for you."

Lucador went back out to the front of the store. "Raine should have stayed," he said to Lucid. "For the show. For the cutting of the air." Lucador liked William's idea of cutting the ether as a social construct. Something for self-empowerment. He was going to add it to his Lodge tonight. "Go make sure William doesn't make the vomit." He changed places with Lucid behind the counter.

The store was filling up. People drinking tea, lingering in the No-Basil Alcove. Buying and snacking on Horror D'Oeuvres. A few minutes later, Kick, then Elijah, arrived to help staff up for Lucador's Lodge tonight.

"Where's Lucid?" Kick said.

"In the back with his dad. The tequila is in charge."

As if beckoned, Lucid approached the counter, a little mopey. "I have to take Dad home," he said. "He just tried to go out the back door."

"Let him go! But you should stay for my Lodge," Lucador said, "and see your successful shepherd lead his flock to victory!"

"He might walk into traffic or something. He needs a bed."

"Go and tuck him in. Make him the cocoa. Sing him the lullaby. Then come back for the entertainment of a lifetime!"

"You don't understand," Lucid said. "I need to make sure he stays in bed."

"Don't make him feel guilty, Luc," Kick said. "Lucid, go take him home."

Lucid left them without another word.

"I would never miss your Lodge," Elijah said, quiet, but eager. "I told Connie my goal is to see every Omniscian, all the regulars at CSE and Omnist II, at least once."

"That's good, good for everybody," Lucador said. "Good for sales when you know the Omniscians."

Lucador helped a customer find a particular board game,

and saw Lucid and William had meandered out of the Forgery. William was distracted by a display of healing stones including amethysts, opals, and agates. He picked up a large purple and white amethyst geode with hundreds of facets in it. He fumbled and nearly dropped it.

"That's my favorite," Lucid said. "It's like half a dinosaur egg. Really expensive."

"Baby Lucid," William said. "Raine, first dress. Geta smiling."

"I see pink and green and purple and red, Dad." Lucid said. "No faces. I wish I saw them. Raine might."

William dragged his hand roughly across the facets. "Crying. Laughing."

"Like father, like son!" Lucador said. "Seeing the words!"

"You're in there, too, right?" Lucid said.

"Not...there." William looked up at Lucid. "Not...here?"

Kick stepped in and tried to get William to set down the geode. People were staring. "Please take him home," he said to Lucid

Lucid took his dad by the arm and began leading him toward the front door.

"Not the front," Kick said.

Too late. William's momentum was downhill through the front of the house.

They were attracting too much attention, so Lucador picked up an animal skin drum and pounded out a slow march for them. "HaHAA!" Make it part of the show. Not weird. But it seemed to draw more attention. People parted the way for their exit, the slow walk of the funereal march.

After they left, the eddies of conversation swirled out to the farthest reaches of the No-Basil Alcove. Customers eyes were alit, like there'd been a celebrity sighting. Random stragglers arrived and joined the hivemind conversation. They were saying the strange man was clothed like he was hiding something. He had a shotgun under his trench coat. He was a vampire killer that hadn't slept in several nights. Maybe he'd been recently bitten. What exactly was wrong with him? He smelled. Maybe he was on drugs.

Lucador weighed the pros and cons of beginning his Lodge early:

Pro: It would shift the conversation back to Lucador again. Forget this William nonsense.

Con: People who arrived on time would now be late and miss the beginning of the entertainment. Everyone deserved to see all of the Lucador Lodge.

Lucador saw Sydnee near the front register. She was always solo. She was wearing a new pin, one that declared her Executive Sainthood at the Emporium. Connie and Kick distributed these as membership awards for big-donor-subscription Consumerians.

"Ah, Sydnee the Lucadorian!" Lucador said.

"I'm an Executive Saint now," Sydnee said. She must have been spending a lot of time at the other location, as well. Lucador needed an Executive Lucadorian pin to rival Connie's. "Where's my Lucid?" she said.

"He'll be back! He took the sick Dad home to give him the soup!"

"That's Lucid's dad everyone is talking about?"

"You missed the opening act!" Lucador said. "Better than the word association!"

Sydnee held up a finger. She was listening to a group of customers next to them. Lucador recognized them as Consumerians who frequented both shops. He bit his tongue.

"The man's possessed!" Becky said. Lucador liked the way she spoke. Very authoritative. "Someone needs to cast out the spirit and give him his old life back."

"It's a shame how society ignores the mentally ill," Ken said. He was naturally quieter. It took the William weirdness to draw him out. "Maybe it's drugs."

"He's not possessed; he's dead," Wilson said. He was a bartender at The Guild. Decent margaritas. Good añejo, too. "It's his own soul that won't leave."

"Guys, guys," Braulio said. He spoke quickly, imploring, all the ideas coming out at once. "He's dead, but he's like a chicken with its head cut off. His body keeps going in its habits for a moment or two. Like kinetic energy. He's trying to act as normal as possible, but he can't because his soul's gone. You all saw. It's too obvious. He was deteriorating right in front of us, in real time."

"You saw that in a movie," Ken said, adjusting his glasses and looking away. This conversation was beneath him. "This is real life."

"Possessed or not, he's going to kill that boy," Becky said.

"It's voodoo," Wilson said. "He's been reanimated against his will."

"So, guys," Kick said to Sydnee and Lucador, interrupting their eavesdropping. Elijah was at his side. "You don't actually think he's dead, too?"

"I think all the things," Lucador said.

"I mean, he can't be dead, right?" Elijah said. "He's just sick. He'll be institutionalized and put on medication and people will move on. Isn't that what always happens?"

"Theoretically," Kick said.

"If he's possessed, I can help with that," Sydnee said. "I've been practicing my exorcism spells. I just did one at home. It worked."

"We could grab our pitchforks and storm their apartment!" Lucador said, kidding, not kidding. "End it like we used to in the old days!"

"I know you're joking, Luc, but I saw him breathing," Kick said. "I can't believe we're even talking like this. You said Raine brought him here? I'll call her."

"William should eat the buffalo jerky," Lucador said. "Protein, iron; soak up the añejo."

TWENTY-SEVEN

27. WILLIAM

The store had been too crowded. Too many people who didn't matter. He'd needed out. The only important people were his children and Geta. He forced himself to breathe while walking, in case anyone noticed. It took a lot of concentration, but the effort would make it look real. But with his mouth open, flies were attracted to his face. He swatted them away, his arm slow like swimming through molasses, and he closed his mouth to force-breathe through his nose. It made a whistling noise, like one or both nostrils were partially clogged.

Then the flies tried to enter his body through his sinuses and ears. Through his pants.

His vision was deteriorating. He'd seen memories of his family in the geode at the shop, little movies that played in his head, but really, he couldn't see the facets of the rock. He felt them. Where were his eyedrops? He still had his sunglasses on, and his eyes were gummy. They'd be itchy if he wasn't so numb. Like breathing, blinking wasn't something he was accustomed to concentrating on. His right eye was the blurrier of the two, and he could only see hazy light through it. He turned his head away from his son and stuck a finger under his glasses and into his eye to remove a glob of cloudy mucus or something. Feeling the softness of the eyeball give against the pressure of his finger made him realize that, even though it didn't hurt, he could scratch his cornea. His eyes were melting. The mucus covered his fingertip, sticking to his dry skin like a tiny oyster. He flicked it off his hand and thought he could hear it splatter on the sidewalk. He almost tripped on the sound.

"Something wrong with your eye?" his son said.

He shook his head, and based on the plane of the sidewalk, his neck was crooked again. He straightened the best he could.

"You sure? I see the words 'blurry' and 'obstruction.'"

"Cross my eyes, hope to blind," William tried to say, but what came out was a couple grunts. He sensed he used to say that when his son was little, but couldn't remember any specific instances.

If he were alone, the flies wouldn't bother him so much. They didn't tickle when they landed on him like they used to. But he didn't want others to notice.

A notification sound came from his son's phone. Finally, a Mote. "Read?" William said.

"It says, 'If no one understands you, you're not really speaking.'"

Sounded like something his daughter would write. She was inside the Omnist, here with them, within his son's phone.

June bugs, or cockroaches, or whatever these beetles were, were so prevalent on the sidewalk here in the evening, that if you weren't careful, they'd scamper over or squish under your shoes. They were feeding on old, dried remnants of jujube berries that had fallen from the trees. They'd rush across the sidewalk like little bolts of black lightning. His son was almost dancing as he walked, avoiding stepping on them with random hops and skips.

But William's feet barely left the ground as he shuffled. Cracks and sections of concrete lifted by tree roots dared him to trip. That and the bugs provided cover for his odd gait.

Once inside the apartment building, William went for the elevator, even though the kids only lived on the second floor. They never took the elevator. His son didn't want to wait for it, but after climbing three steps, he stopped and came back. He must not have wanted to leave William's side. The ancient lifting machine's engine creaked and whined and shuddered to a stop. The doors opened to reveal a black iron cage, which Lucid slid out of the way.

Inside the apartment, his son scooted him to his bedroom and attempted to convince him to climb into the egg-bed. "This will protect you from words," his son said.

Flashback of sleeping bags in the mountains. Hiking to a remote location, then intense, forested darkness. Cold feet. A bear sniffing outside the thin, opaque nylon, less than a foot away from his head. Protect the children.

"And from people," his son said. "It helps."

The carpenter had been explicit about what the bed was. It was more tapered at the feet than the head, like an egg, but also like a coffin. It was the boy's escape pod from spaceship Mother Earth. But now it looked like a blurry casket. A deathly destination. "Bury me," William croaked.

"No, Dad. You told me to help. I'll sleep on the couch."

Flashback to using one arm to snag a small child attempting to flee the room. Caught him running and used the child's momentum to swing him up in the air and around in a circle.

"And I'll guard the door, like you used to do for me," his son said.

He wouldn't be able to sleep, but he couldn't say that. "I'm still alive."

"Like Raine says, if you have to ask, then you have your answer." His son sniffed loudly and made a face. "Maybe you should take a shower first." He pointed over William's shoulders. "'Bacteria,' 'maggots,' and 'odiferous.' You can wash away all kinds of flelling words."

Had William acclimated more to the stench, or had he completely lost his sense of smell?

"I wanted to say something earlier," the boy said, "but I didn't want to embarrass you."

"Okay," William said. He would take a shower. He shuffled across the hall to the bathroom and turned on the water. He put his hand in the flow and felt no temperature, just the pressure of water against his hand. He saw steam puffing a cloud in his face. The wetness felt good on his skin.

"Dad! Are you okay?" The boy pushed him out of the way, felt the water, and adjusted the knob. "I saw the words 'scalding' and 'burning.'"

William put his hand back in the stream. It felt the same.

The boy left the room and William arduously stepped out of his clothes. His coordination was degenerating fast. The sooner he got over this episode, the better. The water would help.

He was constantly dying in his mind. Then constantly reawakening. He was repeatedly experiencing little mental deaths. Reboots. But with each restart, he was coming back with less clarity. Less memory. He felt the memory of repeated deaths more than he remembered the details of the short lives. They were body memories.

He dropped the bottle of his daughter's body soap. It landed on his foot and he felt no pain, only pressure. He bent to pick it up and hit his head on the ceramic wall. This would have been funny several days ago, but now he struggled to stand up again. He managed to straighten a little, enough to pour soap on his head and hold it under the flow of water. It was like wearing mittens for all the dexterity he had.

When he shut off the water and opened the curtain, he didn't know where he was. This wasn't his bathroom; things were in the wrong places. He used a towel rack for balance to step out of the tub. Still bent awkwardly, he scooted into a seated position on the toilet lid and sat there dripping. There was still soap in his armpits and eyes, which weren't burning, and although the mucus had been cleaned out, the soap was causing a swirling cloudy blurriness. He hadn't rinsed well. He used the towel rack to pull himself up.

Someone had taken his clothes and left a robe folded neatly on the sink. He straightened his back enough to put on the robe and inch his way out of the bathroom.

CHAPTER
TWENTY-EIGHT

28. LUCADOR

L ucador waved high and slow at Elijah from just inside the Forgery. He was trying to get his employee's attention. It was time. Lucador was excited for his Lodge, even more so than usual. He'd been inspired by William the Drunkard, Lucid the Word-Boy Wonder, Sydnee the Fair Maiden, and, of course, the fundamentals of all life and death. After dimming the lights, he'd instructed Elijah to run sound and man the spotlight and await his cue. He'd eventually train Lucid to do this, but for now, Elijah would do.

Lucador was cuing in vain. Elijah, not quite a son, but a coworker of the surrogate son, was busy looking at the cute girls. *Focus!* Maybe in the future they would use the GPS-satellite walkie-talkies to communicate like the rebels did in the jungle. Omnist II was a packed jungle tonight, with no spotlight trained on the back of the room.

He finally caught the attention of Elijah, who promptly killed the rest of the house lights, so all that remained was a desk lamp at the register, the exit signs above the front door and the Forgery, and a temperature gauge that reported one of the refrigerators to be a red thirty-six degrees. A lonely spotlight remained trained at the center of the stage.

People applauded and catcalled. They knew what was in store. But they didn't really know what was in store.

"HaHAA!" Lucador began running, clanking out of the Forgery, but the store was so dark and so packed it was difficult to see. He swerved and dodged and bumped into Lucadorians who were in the way. Most had their backs turned to him, facing the stage, not knowing he would run out from behind them. He'd wanted a grand entrance full of energy and surprise, and that was ironically exactly the problem.

"HaHAA!" he said again, less happy but louder, like a car horn, maybe, which sparked more of the crowd to clear him a path.

He made it to the stage and hopped up as if it were a foot taller than it was. He ran into the spotlight, whipped around, and looked expectantly at the crowd. He lifted his eyebrows as high as they could go. His eyes were expressive, bushy, concentric circles—like an owl's.

"Look at you beautiful Lucadorians. You're scared!" He pointed at one, two, three of the Lucadorians looking back at him from the front row. That was as far as he could see with the light in his eyes. At least they were smiling.

"No more talk about people being possessed! I don't want to hear about it!" He could really feel it tonight. Both arms reached for the sky, for the crowd, then pressed into his temples. "No exorcisms, unless you exorcise yourself! Our friend William stopped by earlier and his visit set the talk of Omnist II ablaze!"

This created a stir in the audience. This would have been a great moment for a trick with fire. It took a bigger distraction to distract from a big distraction. Next time. Instead, he paced from one end of the stage to the other, and Elijah dutifully kept the light trained on him.

"Look at this crowd! You're upset...scared...thinking a man is walking around here dead. Think about what you're thinking! Talk about what you're saying!"

The mumbling and buzzing amongst the crowd grew louder. There were a dozen or more side conversations.

"Not now, you fools!" Lucador said. "Now is the time for listening!" He cocked his head as if listening to a distant foghorn. *Another missed cue; a foghorn bit right here would've melted the faces.* He was always amending, adjusting, evolving his Lodges to keep them fresh. "You are the ones who walk around dead! Not him! He's living the best life! He just looks how you feel! William and me, we were playing golf this weekend, sí! Dead people don't chip and putt!"

He pointed at one, two, three Lucadorians again, this time aiming for the most bored-looking of the bunch he could see in the difficult light. "You're dead, and you, and you! You must cut through the malaise!"

Rather than inspiring fear, being called out caused the Lucadorians to smile.

"But you cannot cut, not yet! You need a sword, you say. HaHAA! You've come to the right place!" He had more sheaths and knife holders around his midsection than usual. He unsheathed a sword. It glistened in the spotlight. This pleased him.

"Some swords are made of steel. Some are composite." He showed off a couple fighting stances as he spoke. "I've learned some swords are just made of words, some powerful words. Did you know this? Like good blades, words can be weapons, but the best of them are tools. This one, this is a tool for stabbing and cutting. For making the bleeding. Other tools, you cut the air like you're at war with it."

Lucador lunged, faded, and cut the air. "That is fun, good practice, but when you do that, you're missing the point. You must also clear the air, a path for the words to go!" He planted his feet and swung about him. "Stuck in the muck, you go nowhere with the wrong tool! You're stuck in place with the word-weeds growing all around you. You must clear your way forward!"

He held his sword aloft victoriously with two hands. He sheathed the sword on his belt, went to the side of the stage, and pulled a machete from a hiding place behind a speaker cabinet. "HaHAA! Look at this! A good machete has vision! It's your eyes when you cannot see."

He closed his eyes for effect and imagined slashing his way through the jungles. Banana leaves. Vines. If he projected his visions hard enough, he believed the audience would see what he saw, as well. He opened his eyes and turned the blade in the spotlight, shining the reflected light about the room. *This must look so amazing from out there.*

"It's for forging ahead, to clear your own path!" Lucador looked behind him like he was being followed, then started clearing the air in front of him with the machete, inching his way to the edge of the stage. "Don't look back, no need! It's for others to follow! It's your job to go until you can go no farther."

He looked down, more somber now. "Don't wait for somebody else to save you. I might save you, but alas, there's only one of me! Learn to be the hero of your own life!" He jumped down to the floor.

His mind went blank. He was out of ideas. He'd lost steam. The people right in front of him, right next to him, they were all hanging on his next pronouncement. Usually, he went much longer than this, had more to say. This was almost painful, the loss of words and energy.

"I am done!" he said. "No more words on stage! Come see me to talk. Let's talk about chopping the words, chopping the life into manageable pieces!"

∼

AFTER THE INITIAL rush of Lucadorians had greeted Lucador, several of them wanting photos with him for social media, Sydnee approached and shook his hand.

"That was great!" she said. "One of your best."

"No, no, I've done better." Lucador was practicing modesty. It didn't come naturally. "It was good! They're always good, but I can do better."

"I know what you're doing here," Sydnee said.

"It's my shop. My Lodge. That is not so odd."

"You're talking about Lucid when you talk about words, aren't you?" Sydnee said.

"Lucid is like a son. He doesn't realize what a weapon he is."

"He's a person, not one of your swords, or 'word-swords,' or whatever. You can't forge him in that back room of yours. His dad's sick, so you better treat him extra nice right now."

"I treat him the best! The best there is! He's a good kid. Smarter than me. Smarter than you. But he's also the dumbest person I ever met." Lucador smacked both hands against his sides, causing a succession of rattling noises. "HaHAA! So you better treat him right, too."

CHAPTER
TWENTY-NINE

29. RAINE

"Why aren't you answering your phone?" Raine called out when she entered the apartment. There was no music playing. No television or video games.

Lucid walked out of the kitchen. "It's over there." He pointed to his hoodie, which had been thrown on a couch pillow. It was probably in a pocket.

"First, Olivia's not answering her phone—I've called her three times—and now you."

"You left me to take care of Dad by myself. You should've been there to help."

"I had to go back, but at least Kat's closing." Raine passed Lucid into the kitchen. Dad was in a robe, sitting at the table, staring a little too closely at an open photo album.

214

"He asked if we had any family pictures," Lucid said.

"Has he been talking?"

"Earlier, before he took a shower. Then he got quiet. I think he was reborn."

"I agree. Something in him appears to have died." Raine leaned down, hoping to catch Dad's eye.

"As a compass," Lucid said, "he's no longer pointing a biological north."

Dad got up slowly as if sleepwalking, his robe swinging open.

"Dad!" Raine said. "Close your robe!"

He went to the sink where he started filling up a spray bottle Raine used for the potted palms by the windows in the bedrooms.

"Are you okay?" she asked him.

"Great." His voice rumbled, much more degraded than earlier. He sounded like a dying monster in a movie. He made a throat-clearing sound, then uncoordinatedly misted the inside of his mouth with water. "Never better."

"I brought a tincture for the humidifier," she said. "For your throat. Maybe that'll help. We all need to breathe."

He didn't respond. This was the first time she'd seen him today without the sunglasses and hat. His eyes were tired, blank, lifeless.

"Have you looked in a mirror?" she said.

Still no response. He stared at the wall above the sink.

Raine felt like a mother of two children. "Dad, it's okay. Feelings are real. So yes, you're telling the truth when you say you feel dead. But you have to be alive to *feel* you're dead. Does that make sense?" She wanted to heal him. She wanted to place her hands over his soul, over whatever it was that was aching. His unhappy marriage, his off-center children. Maybe regret about picking career over family. It would take a lot more than just focusing all her heat and energy into her hands.

"Still alive," Dad said.

"Do you think you're dead because you want to be dead?"

"Die."

"That's really serious," Raine said. "Please don't say you want to kill yourself."

"No. Too alive."

It didn't matter that he was making no sense. She just wanted to keep him thinking. Thinking would eventually lead to snapping out of this episode. "We need to get you to the hospital."

No response. William stood in place, staring at the wall.

"Let's get you dressed," Raine said. Still no response. "Where's his underwear?" she asked Lucid.

"His clothes are in the dryer."

"Dad, we need you to go to the hospital," Raine said. "Something's really wrong."

"No." He shuffled back to the table, where he slowly sat down again. "Sleep here. Family." The album was open to a picture of Raine and Lucid as small children. He pressed a finger on it, like he was trying to remember the details. He made happy noises when recognizing Geta, Raine, or Lucid.

"Who?" he said, pressing and smearing a finger on another laminated page. He was pressing on a picture of himself.

"He keeps doing that," Lucid said, as he walked away down the hallway.

"He's in a circular loop," Raine called over to him. "Maybe we can wait until morning, maybe he'll sleep it off. But no later." She left Dad long enough to retrieve sleeping materials out of a closet, placing a pillow and blanket on the couch.

When she came out of the living room, he was no longer in the kitchen. She found him in the bathroom, where he'd pulled out the garbage can and removed a used tampon, and was trying to pull it apart. His coordination was gone and he was fumbling with it, frustrated.

"What's wrong with you?" This was as pissed off as Raine had ever felt. She smacked the item out of his hands.

Dad stood there confused, and Raine got a chill, like he could turn violent any second. Which he'd never been before.

"I'm throwing out the garbage," she said, picking up the tampon and taking the mini wastebasket with her to the kitchen, where she combined it with the garbage there. She sealed up the bag and stood at the entrance to the kitchen. "And if I come back and find you with your hand down the disposal, I'm turning it on." She'd never been violent before, either.

"Dad's still in there, isn't he?" Lucid said from his bedroom. "His shell's protecting him, right? No more colors. He's all grey. No more words flelling around. But his eyes. That's enough to know he's in there, right?"

"Gateway to the soul," she said. Raine left with the garbage bag, down the stairs to the first floor, and out the back door to the dumpsters. A woman was just walking up as she exited, so Raine held the door open for her.

"Thank you," the woman said. She looked familiar. But of course she did. Everyone who lived in the building should look familiar.

"I'm happy to." Raine curtseyed with one arm on the door and one holding a bag of trash. When she returned from the dumpster, the woman was still in the hallway waiting for her. "Can I help you?"

"You're Raine, right?"

"Yes, I'm on the second floor. And you are..."

"Sydnee," she said. "I'm friends with Lucid."

"Oh, you're the infamous Sydnee." Raine had indeed seen

her before at the Emporium. Connie may have recently made her an Executive Saint. "Lucid told me about you guys getting coffee. Come on up."

They walked up the stairs.

"I came up to see him at Omnist II, but they said he'd already left," Sydnee said.

"Of course, he's watching our..." As soon as they got to their floor, she remembered Dad inside. Too late. As long as Dad stayed in the other room and kept his robe closed, maybe Sydnee and Lucid could leave right away. "Our dad's not feeling well."

Lucid was still standing in the apartment's open doorway.

"Sydnee!" he said. He lifted his hand to shake hers, then stopped, took a step forward as if to hug her, and stopped again. Stepped back. This couldn't have been more awkward. Sydnee ended the nonsense by splitting the difference and giving him a one-handed hug, and Lucid tilted his head down, resting the side of his face on top of her hair. He was probably smelling her.

"I didn't know I'd get to meet the family," Sydnee said. "Lucid, can I have a moment with your little sister?"

"Keep an eye on Dad," Raine said. "Just for a moment."

Lucid went back inside.

"I'm the elder sibling," Raine said. "But since he's so much taller, I get that a lot." Sometimes she was still mistaken for being under eighteen. Sydnee looked to be twenty-seven or twenty-eight.

"I want to talk to him about your dad, but I'd like to talk to you first," Sydnee said. "That's all everybody at Omnist II is talking about. Your dad."

Raine didn't want to lay out her entire family health history with a stranger. But here she was. It was better to nip stories in the bud before they grew into something else. "He's having an episode. He sometimes thinks he's dead, and goes out of his way to prove it. We've been convincing him he's alive for years."

"Well, lots of people at Omnist II think he *is* dead. Apparently, he made quite an impression."

"He's getting better at it. He's showered now, but when he was there, he hadn't yet. He hadn't brushed his teeth or changed his clothes."

"Things a dead person wouldn't do."

"Right." But that didn't mean all unhoused people were dead.

"Some people think he's possessed," Sydnee said. "And I'm one of them."

"Did he seem possessed to you?"

"I never got to see him; they'd already left by the time I got there, but from what everyone says, this sounds like a possession. I've seen them in the desert. All-night parties where people welcome spirits to possess them, and they spend all night dancing. When the sun rises, the spirit's supposed to leave the body. But sometimes it doesn't and there needs to be an intervention."

"That's intense and interesting, but there's no way Dad's been out in the desert."

"Well, I'd like to see him; see how much he has in common with Lucid. Being prone to possession can run in the family."

"They're both unique, but they're different from each other. Lucid's seen doctors his whole life. He feels sorry for them, for having to study him, for trying to figure out how his brain works. He says the questions they ask don't always match the words over their heads. But even when he's shut down, he's so full of life and ideas. More so than the doctors he meets. We have little postmortems after appointments where I wonder who's studying whom."

"I think he's just amazing," Sydnee said.

Raine liked that Sydnee's kindness was natural and free-flowing. She felt comfortable with her. "The wonders of the world are indeed wonders," Raine said. "And he has claustrophilia."

"You mean claustrophobia?"

"No, claustrophilia is the opposite. It means he likes confinement or enclosed spaces more than being around people."

"He told me about his egg-bed," Sydnee said. "It sounds amazing."

Raine wasn't sure what the next step should be—if she should invite Sydnee in to see Dad, or go in and switch places with Lucid. "Well, I'm turning in for the night. We're taking Dad to the hospital in the morning."

"What's he doing now?"

"Looking at old family photos in an album."

"I've seen that before. The invasive spirit may be sitting on his memories. When he looks at a familiar photo, a little bit of his old self can resurface."

A glass fell inside the apartment, followed by some shuffling noises.

"Wait, Dad!" Lucid said.

THIRTY

30. WILLIAM

More tunnel vision. More tunnel, less vision.

The boy had given William a vessel of fluid that he didn't want or need. He would regurgitate it if he attempted to consume it.

William stood up, losing his balance. The glass and the plastic book with people in it fell to the floor.

The blurriness of his periphery had been encroaching on the focal point. It wasn't darkness. The light was still there, but everything was cloudy and blurry. It felt as if the walls in the room were pressing against his head and muffling his hearing. He felt air pressure against his eardrums, like his head would implode. He was becoming deaf, too. Sounds were more distant, buried in fluid.

This was the first time he ever thought about trepanation. But it was fleeting thought.

Maybe his brain was rotting.

"Bed," he said. Walking was difficult. Like being drunk on a swerving bus. He moved slowly down the hall, holding the wall to compensate.

"This isn't your house, Dad," the boy said from underwater, with him, but distant. "This is where Raine and I live."

"What words do you see?" the girl said. Her voice was floating above the waterline, but still far away.

"Not many," the boy said. "But there's 'rest' and 'peace'."

"Maybe we should go to the emergency room," the girl said. Footsteps. Another female voice echoed behind her. He smelled different-flavored meat.

"Couch," William said, trying to turn around. The solution was to settle down and not move. "Stay."

He felt a hand on the elbow of his terrycloth robe as he was helped into the living room. Another set of hands tied his robe closed. He sat down on the couch, and felt a different sort of exhaustion, a bonding with nothingness. He leaned sideways until his head rested on the cushions. His neck cracked. He heard it underwater more than he felt it. This was a new sensation.

"Tomorrow," he said. "Sleep."

The shittier he felt, the hungrier he got. The more he tried to stay awake, the more he was disappearing. He could wait until tomorrow. The hospital would feed him. They knew what he needed. An IV of life. Then he'd get proper vision and hearing back. Lying down helped.

"He hasn't slept in a couple days," said the boy. "He's beat."

William closed his eyes and his mind went silent. The light behind the eyelids darkened.

Time passed.

THIRTY-ONE

31. RAINE

I t was late, but Raine had allowed Sydnee and Lucid to remain in the kitchen while drinking an herbal tea blend from the Emporium. She'd asked them to speak quietly, since Dad was finally asleep on the couch. Somehow, dealing with him today made Raine feel unclean, so she jumped in the shower for the second time today.

She always enjoyed the craft soaps from CSE for their unusualness and personality. Sometimes they contained bits of peach pits or blackberry seeds, cinnamon bark or spearmint. Tonight, she scrubbed with an Organica brand pennyroyal and sage soap she had never used before. Bits of sharp herbs and stems scratched lightly and exfoliated her skin. She was removing dead flakes, circulating spent life, pieces of her, back into nature.

She was fortunate to have good skin. People commented

about it. She glowed, not with makeup, but with lotion and vitamins, healthy and vibrant. Her favorite spot was her thighs, where nobody else, not even the sun, ever saw. It was all part of her, and it all mattered.

She used a new Organica lotion, too, one that claimed to nourish the good bacteria on her skin. She was an ecosystem unto herself. She put on her silk sleeping kimono, and checked in on Lucid and Sydnee in the kitchen.

"'Sunwashlegus,'" Lucid said, looking over her head, slowly. At least that's what it sounded like he said. She'd forgotten what he said as soon as he said it. "That's a word." He looked at the table. "I never knew." Lucid was becoming, well, less lucid. He may have been trying to stay awake for Sydnee's sake.

"You're tired," Raine said. "Get some sleep. We have to take Dad first thing in the morning."

"Let me say night, good to Dad," Lucid said.

"He needs his sleep, remember? Don't wake him." It had taken forever for Dad to shut down as it was.

Sydnee leaned over the table and surprised the other two with a kiss on Lucid's cheek, and surprisingly, he didn't melt down. Prior to this, only she and Mom had been allowed that privilege, and even then, it was iffy. Sydnee stayed in the kitchen while Raine and Lucid walked quietly down the hall.

"Shhhh," Raine said. She exaggeratedly tiptoed for Lucid's benefit, even though her own floating walk would have been silent enough.

"Raine?" Lucid said as he climbed into his egg-bed. "You're talking more and more like a regular person. You usually pull the best words from the air, but they're dimming around you now. The words are normal. Like Mom's."

She thought about it and nodded. Something had indeed been changing today. She was experiencing actual stress. Pressure. "Thinking with different words, by definition, means we're thinking differently, right?" she said. *But how much?*

"Are those words gone now?" he said. "No more flelling?"

"I don't know, Lucid. I've never seen the flelling. That's your gift."

"I want to see what words are over Dad right now."

"In the morning," she took a chance and leaned over and kissed his forehead, like a son. They really were equals. But she could also foresee a potential future for him lying out on the couch. That meant she'd spend the rest of her life caring for Dad, then Lucid, and if she were lucky, herself, three flavors in a mixed pack of fruit and herbal soaps. "Night, good."

Lucid slowly pulled down the top of his egg. He liked when Raine pretended to try to open the lid after he closed it, so she gave the wooden escape shuttle a jiggle and imagined him smiling inside, pleased with his protection.

"All safe," she said.

"Don't forget to lock the door," he said softly from inside his egg-bed. She heard him switch on his fan inside.

"I never do," she said, locking it from the inside and backing out of the room.

Raine looked down the hall into the kitchen and signaled to Sydnee to come with her to the bedroom. She closed her door carefully so as not to bother the two sleepers. On the inside of the door was a white posterboard covered in hundreds of quotes written in Raine's handwriting. Hand-written Motes.

"'All you can do is do,'" Sydnee said, reading one. "You wrote these?"

"Lucid's a natural Mote generator," Raine said. "He doesn't think so, but he says many things I feel the urge to write down."

"He says you write the best Motes."

"I do my best. But I was never a fan of using the Omnist to enhance spirituality. I didn't even sign up for the Omnist until I began writing Motes. Connie and Kick are aware of this. Spirituality comes from within, and from how you treat the world and others around you. I just start there."

Sitting on her bed, Raine and Sydnee talked about possessions and exorcisms. Dad would certainly be admitted to the hospital tomorrow, but once he was released, they decided Sydnee should perform an evacuation.

"Not all possessions are evil, mind you," Sydnee said. "Some spirits are just passengers, going along for a joyride in a human vehicle."

"I'd suggest this is more than a joyride," Raine said.

"This possession may be evil because it's harming its host. Or, at minimum, it's exacerbating symptoms of a condition of his. It's a bad combination. Only once the spirit's gone can he truly heal. Until then, the way our society works, he'll only be locked up or medicated."

"You're a healer, too. I can tell," Raine said. "Sometimes Consumerians claim to be healers, but they really just want the attention the word 'healer' brings them. The appearance of being unselfish is itself selfish. How you act in private is who you really are."

Sydnee placed her hand on Raine's. Raine wasn't uncomfortable with touch the way Lucid was. Sydnee's hands were the perfect temperature. Lucid's were often too hot, and Dad's, out there on the couch, seemed cold.

"You're welcome to stay tonight if you like," Raine said. "I have an inflatable mattress I can sleep on and you can have the bed."

Sydnee appeared to consider this. "No, I wasn't even planning on visiting. It just kind of happened when I heard everybody talking at Omnist II." Sydnee paused. "You and Lucid are wonderful. And I should get going."

Raine placed her other hand on Sydnee's. It was like she was consoling *her*, when it easily could have been the other way around. "Lucid has no real friends except for me," Raine said. "And I don't count. I'm family. I know he appreciates that you came by."

"I'm glad I did." Sydnee got up. "Let me know how it goes tomorrow."

THIRTY-TWO

32. WILLIAM

There were indistinguishable voices coming from down the hall. He longed for them, longed for life. He sensed heat from warm bodies. Smelled blood inside them. Food, survival.

Urge to kill—hunger—rising.

Smelled human sweat, blood, flesh.

Sat up cracking. Tiredness replaced by desire. Greed good. Physical greed, a physical need. Fill emptiness.

Shuffled down hallway, bent, broken, tunnel to warm flesh getting warmer.

Door locked. Big shove. All strength, all force. Broke lock.

Food first. Eat first. Hide in coffin.

Warm flesh. Food and safety.

Opening lid.

Hunting. Ancient skills. Natural.

Hunter. No pleasure. Survival. Teat of life.
Not forever. Just not die.
Screaming prey, blood-curdling, annoying, shut up.
Hunger, blood, meat, warm squirming food.
Too many words. Nightmare.
Amber lens. Red lens. Color shift. Monochrome.
No words.

THIRTY-THREE

33. RAINE

*B*oom! The entire building shook with the thundering sound of shattering wood. At night in a quiet apartment, this was unbelievably loud.

"Help! Help!" Lucid screamed from far away, muffled.

Raine got up and pushed past Sydnee, opened her door so fast the Lucid-Motes poster came undone, and ran down the hall to find the door to Lucid's room broken open. She turned on the lights and saw Dad with his hands around Lucid's throat. He was leaning over him, while Lucid was punching and flailing.

"Help! He's biting me!" Lucid's legs were bicycle-kicking, his torso was alligator-rolling. But he was held in place as much by the shape of the bed, the shape of the egg, and Dad's fugue strength.

Raine pulled one of Dad's arms while Sydnee punched him

on the back of his neck. His arm was cold. Dad's flesh was unmistakably dead-grey. Overhead LED lights were horrific on her skin, too, but it was clear now. This man wasn't possessed; he was dead.

While Dad was distracted by the attacking girls, Lucid wrestled out from underneath and rolled onto the floor. Still bent at the waist, Dad reached for Lucid as Sydnee kept punching him on his head, neck, and back. Raine was pulling his arm the opposite direction from Lucid, who crawled far enough away to get on his feet.

"Run!" Sydnee said.

"We can help him, right?" Lucid yelled behind him as he fled the room.

Unbelievable. The man was likely already dead and trying to kill Lucid, and Lucid wanted to save him. Raine and Sydnee gave Dad one final shove over the egg-bed and he fell, hitting his head on the wood of the far side with a sickening crack. Sydnee ran out first, then Raine tried to pull the broken bedroom door closed. It wouldn't latch. She left it. The apartment's front door was open, and Sydnee and Raine ran out to the hallway, down the stairs, and out of the building.

Lucid was waiting for them at the edge of the street. Raine hadn't thought about what direction they should run. Just get away. They went left. Their block was dark and quiet this late on a Sunday night as they ran toward Sunset Boulevard.

Raine was wearing only her silk kimono. No phone, of course. No keys. Lucid wouldn't have his, either. Sydnee's phone was still on the bed in Raine's bedroom. They were nearing Omnist II. Maybe Lucador was still there after his busy Lodge and could call the police.

Raine looked back and saw Dad had finally appeared in the distance, the second story stairs likely slowing him down. He was moving slower than them, not lifting his knees. Lucid was hopping and skipping over skittering bugs, spending much more energy in achieving height versus speed. Sydnee was the only one wearing shoes, but she was staying back to accompany Lucid, or to allow Raine to lead.

Raine could feel the fading lifeforce emanating from the corpses of early summer jujube berries, jacaranda leaves, and other bits of dead organic life forgotten and left to die on the sidewalk. These things were sticking to the bottoms of her feet. The roaches were out in full force tonight, but she managed to avoid landing on any of them, whether alive or dead. The bugs were difficult to see in the near-dark, mixed in with other detritus. She'd heard about locust plagues and prime number broods emerging from underground farther east, but had never experienced bugs quite like this in Los Angeles.

"Did we close the door?" Lucid said.

The door to their apartment was the least of Raine's concerns. The doors to Omnist II, on the other hand, were more important. She got there first, tugged at the handles, and of course they were locked, but some of the lights were still on inside. Someone was there. Raine futilely shook the handles. "Kick!" she said. "Luc!"

Lucador was inside, sitting with a notebook at the counter. He looked up.

Some Lucadorians were loitering on the next street corner, three teenagers, and they'd stopped talking and were looking over to see what was happening.

"Run, you guys!" Sydnee called out to them. "Go home!"

"Okay, Mom!" one of them said, raising a bottle to her.

CHAPTER
THIRTY-FOUR

34. LUCADOR

Aggravated people were at the door. Raine was pulling on the handles and Sydnee was pounding on the glass. Lucid was hopping up and down, doing a pee-pee dance in his pajamas. They must not have keys. *Patience!* Lucador walked around the counter.

"Hurry!" Lucid said.

"Luc!" Raine said. "Open up!"

"Come on, already!" Sydnee said.

All three were barking for him to overcome his apparent ineffectiveness at completing such a simple task. "Horses!" Lucador said. "You think the battle rages!"

He unlocked the door and they all scrambled inside, with Raine slamming and locking the door behind her. Lucid ran straight for the Forgery. Probably for the Omnist Egg.

"Where are the keys?" Lucador said. Raine was barefoot and in a kimono. "And the shoes?"

But she wasn't looking at him, only at the people outside on the corner. "Get out of here!" Raine yelled through the glass. The loitering teenagers were raising their hands, pretending to be upset the trio had been allowed admittance to the store. "Run!" she said, making a shooing gesture.

"Do not yell at the Lucadorians!" Lucador said.

William appeared from the other direction down the sidewalk, lurching toward them, falling forward without falling down, the robe untied and fluttering like a cape. His drunken sense in fashion had taken a disturbing turn for the worse. He tried to open the door. Raine backed up.

"They're closed, man!" one of the kids outside yelled. William redirected his focus and stumbled toward him.

"What the fuck!" one of the other kids yelled. They all ran off in separate directions, with William lurching after one of them.

"Why aren't you calling the police?" Raine said.

"Why do I do that?" Lucador said. "It's King William, paternal of the Oxfords!"

"He's trying to kill us! And now them!"

Lucador hadn't seen any weapon. No yelling. No pounding. Not even making the fists.

"We should've let the others in first," Sydnee said.

Raine looked both ways out the window. "Too late. They're gone."

"Give me the phone," Sydnee said. "I'll call." The cordless was on the counter. Lucador pointed at it. *Calling the police on drunk William!* She picked it up and paced the No-Basil Alcove area while making the call.

It was all coming together for Lucador. This wasn't a drill or a lesson. William wasn't just drunk. "The verdict is in, then, he *is* dead, just like the insightful Lucadorians suspected!" he said. "Death by tequila! All of them knew! It was a town meeting of pitchforks in here! He was good for the business, though. Sold lots of swords." He gestured down the aisle with sword displays, hoping Raine would be impressed by the copious vacancies. She didn't seem to be.

"I'm not concerned with sales," Raine said. Her gears were turning. The Oxfords were thinkers.

"And you missed a great Lodge," Lucador said. "Some say it was the best one yet!"

"Lodges, either," she said, stepping away from the door and looking around as if expecting more people to be present. "Where's Lucid?"

"Probably in the Omnist Egg," he said, mentally patting himself on the back for building such a safe place for the boy to hide.

"Let him recalibrate, then," Raine said. "We'll coax him out when the police arrive."

"The William was quiet and calm when he was here." If Lucador handled Lucid better than the family, maybe he handled William better, too. "The peaceful dead, resting in peace. What did you do to make him want to kill?"

"All life comes from death," she said.

"All peace comes from violence!" Lucador was proud of this one. *Two could play this game!*

"That's not true. But all wakefulness comes from sleep."

"The Oxford riddles never relent," he said. Did Raine ever rattle? "Maybe William tires of them."

Sydnee set the phone back on the counter. "They're on their way!"

There was pounding at the door.

"Oh my god!" Sydnee yelled.

William had returned, and in his fracas with one of the

young Lucadorians, had been left with a chunk of skin hanging off a cheekbone, exposing bone. The boys outside must have defended themselves against the tequila monster, and it was Lucador's turn to protect his people.

"HaHAA!" Lucador's rebel yell sounded more urgent and threatening than ever before. *They will see the serious warrior now!* He drew the more consequential of the two long swords sheathed at his sides and struck a pose. The battle would soon be on. "Open the door!"

"Don't open the door!" Raine said, standing between Lucador and the pounding from the senior Oxford.

"Just wait for the police!" Sydnee said as she ran across the No-Basil Alcove. She wedged herself behind the second stage riser and the back wall. "Come on guys! Out of his sight!"

"The Forgery is safer than out here!" Raine said.

"He flees!" Lucador said as William shuffled away again like a transient. Lucador pirouetted, sword pointing north. Scaring people with a sword, *really scaring them away from battle*, had been a rush he hadn't felt yet. "HaHAA! Who needs the wails of the security alarm? A weapon is more frightening than the loud noise!"

"Maybe he saw a police car," Sydnee said. She looked cozy in her little hiding spot, her head sticking out from behind the riser like a pushup ice cream treat.

"He saw my victorious sword!" Lucador said. "Maybe he thinks twice about fighting against the weapons in here!"

Lucador and Raine walked back to the Forgery and Raine squatted near the Omnist Egg's crawl space entrance. The lights were off, but some light came in from a streetlight in the alley.

"Police are on their way," Raine said to Lucid.

"I don't want Dad to go to jail," Lucid said from inside the Omnist Egg. "Did you lock the door?"

"Lew-said-door! Lucidor!" Lucador said. How had no one thought of this? "HaHAA! The wordsmith Oxfords missed one. Lucid and Lucador are now as one! The *two* musketeers. The Lucidor!"

"The door!" Lucid said. "Raine! Is it locked?"

"It is, indeed," Raine said.

"I have a sword, and let's get you one, too," Lucador said. "A sword for—" Lucador sounded out the new word softly— "Lew-said-door. Come, come!" Lucador patted the top of the Omnist Egg. Its three loosely attached sections shook loudly. "You can come out. We are all locked up in here!"

Lucid didn't crawl out of the Omnist Egg.

"Regardless, I will find," Lucador said, sheathing his sword and walking into the main room. He browsed through the depleted display of swords, looking for one that was appropriate for a novice. Clusters of them were locked to the display unit by cable bicycle locks. The metal on metal clanked pleasantly.

"Not so many left, but I'll find you the one to keep!" Lucador announced to the hiding Lucid. "You should all take swords! Take the lessons!"

"I hear something. He's out there," Sydnee said, out of sight. Probably still in her hiding place. "He's coming back."

"Do you see him?" Raine said.

"I can see the words," Lucid said, standing now at the entrance to the Forgery. He'd left his hiding place. Time to be a man! "I see 'run,' 'flee,' 'escape,' 'pain,' and 'death,'" he said.

"HaHAA! I knew it! I knew this was the one!" Lucador scrolled the four-digit code on the bicycle lock, Omnist II's street address, and removed a sword. "Yesterday, you wrote the card! It knew before the sword knew! And now you know!"

But before he could hand the sword to Lucid, there was an explosion of crashing glass from the front window. William had thrown a box planter through the glass door. He stumbled through the open space and headed for them.

Lucador jumped to life, and in one motion hopped onto the back of a couch, posed with this new sword, and valiantly jumped down and struck William dead in one fell swoop.

Except that in his rapid departure, he'd actually bumped into the sword display, causing a loud half-dozen sword-slide, and as he leapt, the new sword's hilt had caught on one of his puffy sleeves, and while distracted and not quite jumping high enough, he tripped over the couch, falling flat on his face next to the spot William had just been. William lurched toward the Forgery's entrance, where Lucid had just been, and disappeared inside.

As Lucador scrambled to his feet, there was a loud crash and slide of metal in the Forgery. He suspected the source. At the entrance to the back room, Lucador saw William had collapsed the Omnist Egg into its three pieces and was pulling Lucid out of the wreckage by a foot.

Lucador lifted his sword and was about to strike, the valiant knight beheading William Oxford. William looked at him with fire and white, survival and fight, in his eyes.

A single strike, and Lucador sliced the neck clean through, William's head bouncing once and rolling to a stop, facing him.

"Aauugghh!" William said, head still attached to his body, still looking at him, hands reaching for Lucid's neck.

Lucador hadn't actually swung his sword. He'd envisioned it. Two times in a row! He'd hesitated. The worst mistake a soldier could make. As much as he wanted to strike William down, murder was murder. Even murdering a dead man.

"Aauugghh!" Lucador replied, punching at William's collarbone with his sword's hilt.

This distraction was enough for Lucid to flail and squirm out of William's grasp, and tug at Lucador's pant leg. Lucador lifted Lucid with one arm and pushed William again with the other. William fell awkwardly into the wreckage of the Omnist Egg.

While William was struggling to get up, Lucador stood in a full iron gate guard, both hands on the sword lowered between his legs, angled and ready to strike.

"It is time!" Lucador said. *The time for warriors to be made! Time to kill a dead man! No more hesitating!*

Lucid stepped in front of Lucador. "Stop! Colors are changing!" he said. He placed a hand on Lucador's hilt. When Lucador removed a hand to push Lucid out of the way, Lucid tore the weapon away from him and tossed it on the ground. *The boy, not a boy, he's Lewis now, and much stronger than he looks.*

"And that isn't what you think it is," Lewis said, pointing at the floor. "It's just a word, the word for 'sword.' We have to help my dad!"

"He's already dead, Lewis!" Lucador said.

"It's not your dominion," Lewis said.

William, on his feet again, grabbed Lewis by the collar from behind. They wrestled and fell to the floor. Metal noises. Lucador nearly fell over when they rolled into his legs. He grabbed William's bathrobe and hair, pulling his head back. People should be hot, humid, especially after running and fighting. William was cold.

"The words, Lucid, the words!" Raine said from somewhere behind them.

"Unmutem-mutus, William Raymond Oxford!" Lewis yelled. "Bulword-oxifus!"

Then William's body separated from his head, the mass of body collapsing to the side. Lucador was left holding the separated head by the hair. Lucid was holding the sword in its place and breathing heavily. The blade was mere inches from Lucador's face.

"It's my dominion!" Lewis said, confident and forceful.

The story card had known. The sword had known. The boy had known. Why hadn't the warrior?

There was disturbingly little blood to drip. Lucador placed William's head onto the decapitated body reverently and helped Lucid up. The way William's body lay to the side of the remnants of the Omnist Egg, it looked like he was spooning a piece of it.

"Your words," Lucid said weakly, shy again, and tired. "Cut your losses." He bared his upper teeth at Lucador.

Raine embraced Lucid. Sydnee patted Lucador on the back, and he patted her in return. He may have patted her a little too hard, based on the strange face she made. Then Sydnee hugged Lucid.

"What is that?" Lucador said to Lucid, mimicking baring his teeth. "Why do you make that face?"

"He was showing you his egg tooth," Raine said.

CHAPTER
THIRTY-FIVE

35. RAINE

The police arrived, and Omnist II was now officially a murder scene. This was the second time in a year a death had occurred at one of Connie's properties.

When Raine was able to break away from questioning for a moment, she called Mom from the store's landline. Her own phone was still at home. Mom told her she'd try calling Olivia, too, but Raine suspected it would go straight to voicemail. This wasn't right. Maybe Dad had killed her first.

A police officer across the room ended a call on his phone. "Raine Oxford?" he said.

"You may call me Raine," she said.

"We have word on Olivia Oxford; she was William's wife?"

"Yes."

"She was in a car accident Friday night and is currently admitted at St. Joe's hospital in Burbank. She might still be in a coma. William is believed to have been driving the car, but fled the scene."

That would've been after the party. That's what happened to Dad: He'd been dead for forty-eight hours. Some "golf injury."

As the media arrived, officers brought the four of them—Raine, Lucid, Sydnee, and Lucador—down to the police station. At least they avoided the questions from reporters.

Technically, Lucid was arrested under suspicion for murder. He was handling this all surprisingly well. Staring catatonically came naturally to him. They all spent the evening giving their testimony. Raine, Sydnee, Lucador, and Omnist II's security tapes were all witnesses to Lucid's self-defense. Even the kids who'd had a scuffle with Dad out front of Omnist II would be able to corroborate his homicidal behavior once the police tracked them down. Lucador knew at least two of their names.

Lucid was the only one who needed to post bail, and Mom did so once she was permitted. The legal process was certain to take months, but they were reassured if all the evidence lined up the way it appeared to, no charges would be filed.

TWO DAYS LATER, Raine and Lucid were in a waiting room at St. Joseph's hospital. They'd been told Olivia had just come out of her coma, and were waiting for permission to enter her room. Raine wasn't going to ask Lucid what colors he saw, or what words were flelling around the waiting area. He was probably doing his best to ignore whatever extrasensory things hung out in hospitals. He was wearing figurative sunglasses and blinders and pulling at his hair mindlessly. It didn't look stressful; he was just busying himself.

"Why did you say Dad's name at the store," Raine said. "You know, when..."

"I saw his name mingling with Mutables," Lucid said, as if this were obvious. "They were really close together, like they were trying to tell me something. I'd never seen that before. By saying his name with the nearest Mutable, they joined and disappeared together."

"The word was nonsense. Do you remember it?"

"I don't. But they're never nonsense. Don't ever say that about a word. It was a Mutable. It existed only for that moment. In that place. Its purpose was to save me, and once I said it, it was gone."

She couldn't remember the exact word either. Only the part with Dad's name. She also couldn't remember if she'd ever heard Lucid say a Mutable out loud before, but she supposed she had. By definition, she could never remember it. "So, his soul left with the Mutable?"

He acted as if he hadn't heard her. Why would a soul depart with an unspeakable word? Would it have made more sense if Dad had died here—correction: lost his soul—in the hospital, in a spiritual airport with ringing bells and people dressed in white?

They sat in silence for a few minutes. Hospitals were the dirtiest sterile places in the world. The loudest quiet spaces. The most stressed-out sources of respite. The most religious sites of science. Here, nonbelievers believed, and the most pessimistic held out hope.

"I take it you're a dualist now?" Raine said. But it wasn't gloating. She just wanted to hear him say it. The soul had separated from Dad's body.

"No," Lucid said.

Raine wondered if Lucid ever went bald, what he would do

with his hands while he reflected on his interior world. Would he pick and poke at his scalp?

"The Mutable was a specific word of strength," he said. "It was a one-time gift from the universe to me, to help me overcome my fear to fight for my life. I accepted the help of those who flell for my sake. It's difficult to describe, as we don't have the right words for it."

"But didn't you say Dad's soul attached to a Mutable and moved on with it?"

"No, his soul was nearly gone already. It was disintegrating with his body. By cutting off the head, I killed whatever last bit of him was left, and it was that last bit that was trying to kill me."

She wanted to say Dad didn't really want to kill him, that no father wanted to kill his son, but that would be a blatant lie. She, Sydnee, and Lucador had all been witnesses.

"He believed my existence ruined his life," Lucid said.

Dad may have indeed felt that way, but he'd been misaligned, broken for years. Nobody else harbored negative feelings about Lucid, not Raine, or Mom, or the grandparents. Not Lucador.

A nurse waved at them from the hallway door. "Oxford?" she said.

Mom, Ryan, and the Oxford grandparents joined the children in Olivia's room as if they'd always been blood family. Members of Olivia's side of the family were to arrive later in the day. Mom had never treated Olivia rudely. Never acted jealous or dismissive toward her. Her concern for Olivia's well-being was genuine.

Olivia was largely still in shock and weak from medication. A doctor had already broken the news earlier that Dad had died, and the family members performed great feats of mental contortion to keep the conversation about the suddenness and sadness of the tragedy, not how he'd died. How he was a beloved son and father, and partner in a successful accounting firm. Also not mentioned was how he'd been a stranger with a father's sense of responsibility. Or a father with a stranger's sense of family.

After a while, Olivia steered the conversation toward mundane, everyday things. The comfort of the banal. She asked Lucid how he liked working at Omnist II. She was happy for him. He was now officially an adult.

"Makes me think a lot," he said, placing his hand on the bed's railing. His clothing had a variety of red and purple hues today. He was also the only one in the room who wore his everyday expression on his face. Everyone else was more somber and solemn than normal. Lucid was Lucid.

"It's a different kind of thinking," he continued. "Organizing and sorting and counting. I make games with numbers, barcodes, prices, and pricing. I know the unit costs of nearly everything."

"You sound like William," Olivia said.

"Yes, it's an erotic activity," he said.

The room stopped on a dime. Quiet, but charged. Did Mom stifle a laugh? Were there things about Dad they couldn't talk about?

"You're saying that again," Raine said. She was mortified. Had to save him. Lucid could talk openly about anything with her, but he apparently still needed work on his boundaries in mixed company. "I'm afraid you either don't know what the word 'erotic' means, or you have a deviation we haven't talked about yet."

Grandpa Lewis beamed like he'd recently been talking with Lucid about watching pornography. Olivia laughed softly, her eyes brightening. Kids. This was Lucid's way of reminding everybody, gainfully employed or not, that he was still socially a child.

"Erotic? Ewww," Lucid said. "I said 'neurotic.' It's a *neurotic* activity. I can *dwull*...and *swum*...in *num*bers..."

Olivia lifted an arm attached to an IV and placed it on Lucid's hand. Of course that's what he meant. And if he hadn't, it was a hell of a kick save. He patted Olivia's hand in return and then backed away, likely long past his threshold for human contact, and allowed the senior members of the family to talk about family things.

Had Dad loved Geta and the children? Yes. Had he known how to handle that emotion or display that affection? No. Had he loved Olivia? Raine didn't know for sure, but she assumed yes, as well. As William's brain and, as Lucid would argue, his soul deteriorated, Olivia, who'd been the most recent addition to his life, was also the first one he seemed to forget. He eventually lost words, the names, for Raine and Lucid, and stopped recognizing himself in photos. After the accident, he'd mentioned work to them exactly zero times.

ON THE WAY HOME, Raine was feeling more like her old self again. Seeing Olivia on the mend had helped, as well as a welcome return of the airy whimsical thoughts about the universe and humankind's place in it. She missed her dad, of course, but in a way, he'd been dead for years. She didn't think about this without compassion, just that there was less to miss about him as an adult than there would have been when she was, say, ten years old. She didn't want him to die, but had to accept what the universe had brought them. Car accidents happened. And she was more confident now that Lucid could take care of himself, even live alone, if he needed to.

She didn't receive a lot of texts. But she heard her phone buzz and saw a notification from Jacob. Maybe he wanted to redeem the raincheck on getting out, maybe dinner this time. He didn't know about Dad yet. That would be a longer conversation, and one she wanted to have out of her brother's earshot.

Lucid was tapping out a jazz rhythm on the passenger window. He was in a startlingly good mood, as if they hadn't just spent hours in a hospital. His effort to block out bad frequencies and aggressive words and colors there must have been successful. He looked at his phone. "I got a Mote earlier. 'Interdependence inspires exponential destiny.'"

"Yup," she said. The siblings were destined to remain close?

"Doesn't sound like you this time," he said.

"I think that's one of Kick's. But it still counts as predictive, as I was thinking along those lines." Or something.

"Me too," Lucid said.

"Do you think you could write Mutable Motes?" she said. "Like, as soon as it's read, it disappears? The question would be if the meaning remained in your head after the words disappeared."

"I don't know. Mutables arrive on their own terms; I can't conjure them. I haven't tried to write them down, either. In real time, I guess. I bet I would have to write them letter by letter, not sounding out the words. Otherwise, they may evaporate before they're recorded."

After a minute or so, "Do you think Dad's memories and soul were disappearing together?" Lucid said.

"What do you mean?" she said.

"Just, do you think he remembered going to Omnist II, being at our apartment? Did he remember when we were born?"

"I think he was left with a different sort of memory. Like emotional or psychic."

"Like muscle memory?"

"Muscle memory of the soul." That sounded like the title of a self-help book Kick would make fun of, but then order a box of to sell at the stores. "I think the extra couple days Dad had was a gift, an opportunity to see life through different lenses before passing on. He was dead, but aware. People used to dig up bodies and drive stakes through their hearts or chop off their heads for fear of reanimation. They were killing the dead. Maybe they had good reason. Maybe there's a recessive reanimation trait some people are affected by."

"If it's a genetic trait, then you and I may have it. There can be so much life after death," Lucid said. "Does that mean you'd rather be cremated?"

"No. If I were stricken with extended sentience, I'd want to spend that time considering my life lived. Even in a coffin buried in the dark. I wouldn't be able to get out, but I also wouldn't need to."

"I bury myself alive every night. I think it sounds peaceful," Lucid said.

"I do, too. But you wouldn't really be buried alive. Your body's already dead, and you'd have no need for light or air or food. I imagine it would be really peaceful and quiet."

"Heaven. If our life is the creation of our mind, building from nearly nothing at birth, then death is the fading out of our soul. Death would be like meditating yourself to sleep."

They seemed to agree on that part. A dark, thoughtful, peaceful transition from life to death. And this would be the most important and final meditation of Raine's life. Then her soul would separate from her body and she'd carry on with her newfound lessons. But Lucid would say this final meditation faded into darkness, to nonexistence, to eternal sleep.

"If words exist outside us," Raine said, "then words like 'life' and 'death' are hollow until they land on someone."

As they parked, Lucid looked around like he was following a bug flying around the inside of the car. "A Mutable. I ignomember that." He removed his seat belt and opened the door, seeming to watch something invisible flell out of the car.

"Ignomember?" Raine said. "Is that what you said? Did you find another new word?"

"Sort of. Who knows how many times I've found it? It's like remembering to forget, and then forgetting. It's a word that you don't know you knew once, because by definition you then forgot. We just don't know how often it's been used."

Today someone must've swept the sidewalk of the jacaranda leaves and old dried jujube berry remnants. An entire galaxy of little purple spots speckled the concrete, and would remain until the rain months from now washed them away.

Raine's keys jangled in the lock of the building as she opened it.

"You'll forget," Lucid said, jogging up the one flight of stairs. "We always do. We've discovered, then lost the concept of unknown unknowns thousands of times."

"What am I supposed to forget?" she said, tossing her hemp bag on the couch. She wouldn't forget to call Jacob. It was time. They had so much to talk about. And she was teasing Lucid; he was an adult now. He could take it.

The expression on Lucid's face suggested he was seeing a Mutable, or communing with a colorfast pun. As far as she knew, he was the only human capable of this, mixing frequencies and wavelengths in his mind to make new colors, new visual jokes. Jokes she'd never get.

ACKNOWLEDGMENTS

I've talked the ears off too many people to acknowledge them all here, but here's a bunch of them:

Becky Abeita, Nick Allen, Eric Augustine, Kelly Bashar, Burton C. Bell, Debra Bemis, Nicole Bemis, Caeri Bertrand, Jackie Beville, Matt Beville, Rohan Bhagwandas, Morgan Brandon, Ashley Carlson, Debra Clark, Michael C. Clark, Tim Clark, Caroline Concha, Adam Conner, Carmelo Conti, Eddy Contreras, Christa Cooley, Jill Cordova, Christian Draheim, Geo Donaires, Angela Duarte, Thomas Duffy, Angi Dyste, Erik Elhert, Stephen Ellis, Tony Essa, Bryan Fetner, Josh Forge, Kiki Franklin, Ruben Garcia, Derenik Gharakhanian, Joe Glading, Ken Gombos, Brian Graves, Mercedes Graves, Annie Green, Travis Greene, Aaron Guerra, Mike Halloran, Anne Harting, Lee Harting, Leandra Hays, Nick Hays, Keith Hershey, Georgia Hesse, Ken Holt, Avily Jerome, Alexis Jones, Allyson Jones, Ryan Keleher, Richard Kent, Stefanie Kent, Amanda Kibiloski, Erin Killean, Grant Knox, Erin Kruse, Scott Kruse, Anne Lane, Kyle Lane, June Low, Sean MacDonald, Scott Maginnis, Ben Marks, Buffy Marley, Peter Marley, Erik Marshall, Nachie Marsham, Wilson Martinez, Sean Mason, David Mastros, Sonja Mastros, Tim Mayse, Katie Mayo, Melissa McCabe, Matt McCracken, Michelle McCracken, Sean McGoldrick, Carlos Mendiola, Uriel Mejia, Frank Merle, Nick Merrick, Brett Merritt, Kathis Merritt, Allison Meyerhardt, Brittany Meyerhardt, Joe Mikan, John

Mitchell, Chino Moreno, Dan Murphy, Adam Murray, Bekki Newton, Dave Newton, Amy Nichols, Braulio Ochoa, Eileen O'Connell, Chris Ostray, Brenna Otts, Kat Paled, Jessica Parker, Max Pastor, Erwin Payez, Andrew Phillip, Robert Phillips, Ken Pittenger, Denise Pleune, Jacob Plsek, Jeff Prosser, Courtney Ramshaw, Jane Asher Reaney, Joy Robins, Chris Saksa, Dennis Scheyer, Rohner Segnitz, Scott Shiflett, Julie Smith, Clay Speicher, Dustin Stanton, Helen Stanton, Jodi Tack, Phyllis Tesoro, Carl Thomas, Christy Timmons, Christian Townsend, Mike Welchans, Azul Weldon, Ed Weldon, and Tony Yanow.

About the Author

Rob Weldon lives in Los Angeles, CA, and works at a craft beer bar. To learn more about his books or to connect, find him online at: Facebook.com/theomnistseries, Mastodon @Rob-Weldon, or Instagram: @blood.wren.

www.ingramcontent.com/pod-product-compliance
Lightning Source LLC
Chambersburg PA
CBHW022036240626
47154CB00007B/2426